The Obstinate Murderer

To Frank E. Blackwell

© 2013
Cover © Bryce Pearson

Black Curtain Press
P.O. Box 632
Floyd, VA 24091

ISBN 13: 978-1627555463

First Edition
10 9 8 7 6 5 4 3 2 1

The Obstinate Murderer

Elisabeth Sanxay Holding

I

Cleef sat in the hotel bar, alone and at peace. It was eleven o'clock on a June morning; the sun was bright gold behind the Venetian blinds; the little bar was dark and cool; the sound of traffic in the street outside was too familiar for him to notice. He lit another cigarette and turned his head to signal the bartender. The man wasn't there.

That did not matter. At noon, or a little before, fellows he knew would begin coming in, and he would have drinks with someone. With anyone. He moved over to a leather divan in a corner and stretched out his long legs; in this dim light he looked boyish, lean and powerfully-built and nonchalant. But when he struck a match, the little flame showed the lines about his good-humoured mouth and his tired eyes; his fair hair was growing thin at the temples. It had taken him forty years to become what he was.

"Another Scotch, Mr. Van Cleef?" asked the bartender, suddenly appearing beside him.

"Okay!" said Van Cleef. After the first couple of drinks in the morning, which were badly needed to pull himself together, he was no longer impatient, but he refused no suggestions.

"Going away over the week-end, Mr. Van Cleef?"

"Couldn't say," answered Van Cleef. For that, too, depended on other people's suggestions. It was Friday now; if someone got after him, he would pack a bag and go—somewhere. If he were not got after, he would do nothing.

"Beginning to feel like summer," the bartender observed.

"What is it, boy?"

"Telephone for Mr. Van Cleef," said the bell-boy, and Van Cleef got up, and went leisurely out into the lobby, and into a booth.

"Mr. Van Cleef?" said a familiar enough voice.

"Emilia..." he said. "Hello, my dear girl. How's everything with you?"

"Arthur, I've got to see you!"

He glanced around him, as if the booth had become a trap.

"Certainly, my dear girl! Why not come in to dinner-lunch—?"

"I can't," she said. "Can't you come out here, Arthur? It's very serious.... Arthur, I'm being blackmailed!"

"What!" he cried. "But—Yes, of course. Yes, I'll come, Emilia...."

"At once, Arthur?"

"Oh, yes!" he said. "Certainly, my dear girl."

Hanging up the receiver, he went immediately to the bar; it seemed providential that there was a drink standing on the little table waiting for him.

"Blackmail," he said to himself. "Extraordinary girl.... What put that into her head, I wonder?"

Sipping his drink, he fell into a reverie, melancholy and resigned; a voice spoke his name so gently that it scarcely disturbed him.

"Mr. Van Cleef!"

He looked up, to see a boy standing beside him, an extraordinarily handsome boy, slim, almost slight in build, with a dark narrow face, brilliant with life.

"I'm Russell Blackman," he said. Said it with a curious eagerness; as he stood there, hat in hand, he had the look of one imploring a favour.

"Sorry..." said Van Cleef, with an apologetic grimace.

"Don't you remember me?" said the boy. "You knew my Aunt Hilda—"

"Yes," said Van Cleef, sitting up straight. "Yes. Sit down, Russell. Have a drink?"

"Thanks," said Russell. "Just ginger ale, please."

"Ginger ale, and another Scotch," said Van Cleef, without looking at the waiter beside him; he was staring before him. "Yes," he said. "I remember your Aunt Hilda."

"Then don't you remember me? When they realized how ill she was, they sent me off to board at the day-school I went to. It was in the Easter holidays; nobody else there. It was the first time I'd been away from home, and it was hell. I didn't know what to do with myself. I felt—forgotten. And then you came, in your car. You brought me a steamer-basket full of cakes and chocolates and fruit, with a big silver gauze bow on the handle."

Van Cleef glanced sidelong at him.

"Ten years ago..." he said.

"Yes. I was eight then."

"And you've remembered, all this while?"

"I don't forget much," said Russell.

Van Cleef shifted his big shoulders, so that he could look more easily at the boy.

"When my aunt died, you came again,? said Russell. "You drove me home and you talked to me."

"I remember. You were a queer little kid. Excited—"

"I was a freak," said Russell, with a sudden, almost spasmodic smile.

"I don't know.... Just a queer kid. Found you walking up and down in a big, overgrown garden like a jungle-pouring rain—arms folded behind you like a little Napoleon...."

"I was a freak," said Russell again. "They took me out of school that year. I went ahead too fast. I had tutors at home, and there was a great effort to get me interested in sports. I went in for swimming and tennis, and got all the junior cups. And still I was ready for college before I was fourteen. My people sent me abroad with a fine, wholesome young man for a tutor. We climbed mountains. We made walking tours with knapsacks. He did his best; it wasn't his fault that I picked up three languages."

"Bitter..."

"Not any more," said Russell. "I've got past that."

"Have you?" said Van Cleef, looking at him with his tired eyes narrowed.

"Once you accept the fact-that you're a freak," Russell went on, "there's considerable stimulation in finding that you're entirely alone."

"No family?"

"Mother and father, a sister, a brother, uncles, aunts, cousins, and so on. But they've let me go now. I get an allowance of four hundred a month—"

"That's a hell of a lot, at eighteen."

"My parents feel guilty because they don't like me," said Russell. "It eases their conscience to give me plenty of money. And I have no vices. I don't even smoke."

"What do you do?"

"Nothing."

"College?"

"I tried it, for a month. But I wasn't what you'd call popular, either with my fellow-students or the professors."

"Where d'you live?"

"Here," said Russell. "I just moved in to-day. As soon as the home ties were broken, I started looking for you. And when I found you here, I took a room."

Van Cleef took up his glass, and stared at it.

"Mistake..." he said.

"How?"

Van Cleef smiled, his curiously gentle smile.

"Ten years..." he said. "People change, in ten years."

"You haven't changed," said Russell.

"My God!" said Van Cleef, setting down the glass. He looked at Russell, and the boy's black eyes met his steadily.

"I've got my car here, Mr. Van Cleef. What about driving out to the country for lunch?"

"Oh! The country?" said Van Cleef, with a start. "I've got to go out to Blackhaven for the week-end."

"I'll drive you out."

"Good enough!" said Van Cleef, rising. "I'll go up and pack a bag."

"Can I help you?"

That smile came over Van Cleef's lined face again, half rueful, infinitely good-humoured.

"No... No, thanks," he said. "Can do."

"What time will you be ready?" Russell asked, but the other had already turned away; he crossed the lobby with his loose-jointed stride, his broad shoulders a little bent; he got into the elevator and went up to the top floor. He had a suite there; the sitting-room was in perfect order, shades drawn half-way down, furniture stiffly arranged, a room as impersonal as it had been when he had come into it two years ago. Nothing belonging to him except a few books on shelves built into a corner, and a radio.

The chambermaid was in the bedroom.

"Don't mind me, Nelly," he said. "I've got to pack. Happen to see a bag around?"

She was stout and middle-aged, and competent; she knew Mr. Van Cleef's ways. She found the bag for him, and, in a persuasive fashion, she got it packed for him.

"Don't bother, Nelly!" he kept saying, and she kept answering, "No, sir," while she opened the bureau drawers, got out clean shirts, pyjamas, socks, underclothes, handkerchiefs. A very neat gentleman, Mr. Van Cleef was, and all his things were of the best. Very neat; no trouble at all, and so very kind....

"I hope you have a good time, sir," said Nelly.

But somehow she didn't think he would. Somehow, he looked sort of sad, so neat in his dark blue suit and his well-polished brown shoes, standing there and looking at himself in the mirror.

"Hilda..." he said to himself. "My God.... Ten years.... So damned long.... Yet, in another way, so damned short.... Like one day.... I must be indestructible.... Asbestos lining.... Only not the soul. Poor little dried-up soul, rattling around inside somewhere.... Come in! Come in!"

A bell-boy took his bag, and they descended together. Van Cleef looked into the bar; Russell was not there.

"I'll wait a bit," he said to the bell-boy, and sat down on a sofa in the lounge. "Queer kid, this Russell," he thought. "Hard to say whether he needs a kick in the pants, or a little kindness.... Hilda wouldn't like him. Very intolerant girl. But she had every right to be. She was an angel, and angels don't have to put up with anything. Such a fierce little angel.... *That's* that!"... She wouldn't like me, any more.... She never liked me, much. Just loved me."

"Ready?" asked Russell.

"Ready, aye, ready!" said Van Cleef, and they went out into the brilliant sunshine. "That's a good car," said Van Cleef, stopping to examine the roadster. "A very good car."

"They don't come any better," said Russell.

The boy was a master driver, but arrogant.

"It seems to me you're one of these roadhogs," said Van Cleef. "You worried the good lady in the Ford."

"I don't cultivate consideration for others," said Russell.

"Kiddish."

"No. It's biologic."

"Meaning you're the superior animal? Well, no.... I don't think so."

"Superior in cunning," said Russell.

"Q.E.D.," said Van Cleef.

They got out of the city traffic, on to a parkway; the indicator showed fifty, sixty, seventy, eighty.

"Too fast for you?" asked Russell.

"No," Van Cleef answered, agreeably. "If it's a traffic cop, you'll be the one to pay or go to jail. And if we both break our necks, there won't be many mourners, eh?"

"The question is, if death is worth dying. It may be the great experience—the big thrill. But suppose it isn't? Suppose it's—nothing?"

"More kiddishness."

Russell slowed down the car.

"I wish to God you'd talk to me," he said, unsteadily. "I've been waiting ten years to get back to you. I've been thinking of you, all that time, as the only human being I've ever met."

"What d'you mean? Must be plenty of human beings—"

"No! You don't even know what I mean."

"I don't. I'm sorry," said Van Cleef, disturbed. "I don't."

"Let it go," said Russell. "I can't explain."

But Van Cleef was troubled now, with a dim oppression of guilt.

"Failed him, some way," he thought. "Thing is, what did he expect? What was I, ten years ago? Someone different? Probably. I'm sorry," he said, aloud. "Look here! Suppose we stop for a bite of lunch? There's a decent-looking place."

Without a word, the boy turned into the drive-way of an inn, and Van Cleef looked at him anxiously. His profile was extraordinarily fine, subtle in modelling, intelligent, but so very young. The smooth olive cheek had a downy look; the line of the jaw was still rounded.

"May be mistaken about himself," thought Van Cleef. "Certainly he's not average, but he may not be as wonderful as he thinks he is. We'll hope not."

They found a table on the glass-enclosed veranda of the inn, and the waiter came to them with an enormous menu.

"Always wonder at these things," said Van Cleef. "They couldn't have all these items ready, could they? Duck, chicken, turkey, lobster, crab, sole, nine vegetables.... But also they couldn't *get* 'em ready in time, if anyone ordered them...."

Russell spoke to the waiter, in a foreign tongue; the waiter's face lit up; they talked volubly.

"He recommends the broiled lobster," said Russell.

"I'll trust him. But in the matter of drinks—tell him to bring along a bottle of Scotch. Unopened."

The waiter went off, and Van Cleef lit a cigarette, leaning back in his chair; he gazed thoughtfully out across the lawn; he did not look at Russell, he asked no questions.

"Do you know any Greek?" asked Russell, presently.

"No. Oh, no...."

There was a long silence; the waiter came with a bottle of whisky, and opened it; he spoke in his own language to Russell, but got only a brief answer.

"You're not going to encourage me in showing off," said Russell. "Quite right."

Van Cleef glanced at him, and sighed. Then that smile came over his face.

"That was the idea," he said.

"Why?" Russell demanded vehemently. "For God's sake, why be so grudging? I don't expect you to like me, but why do you feel it's necessary to belittle me? If it were anyone but me, you'd have asked what language I was speaking, and how I learned it, and so on. But because it's me, it's irritating."

Van Cleef poured himself a drink.

"Well.... D'you have to be like this?" he asked, with anxiety.

"Yes, I do. I thought you'd understand."

There was another silence.

"What are your plans?" asked Van Cleef.

"I haven't any."

"What are you going to do with yourself?"

"I could be a doctor," said Russell. "I could be a chemist. I could be a zoologist, a lawyer. I could be a financier. There are plenty of careers open to me. I don't want any of them. I'm trying to find—something to want."

"It's possible to live without wanting anything much," said Van Cleef. "I do, y'know. But at your age, maybe it's not possible."

"Is that your advice? Renounce ambition, stop wanting anything—"

"I'm not giving advice. I'm talking, that's all."

There was a flicker of uneasiness in the boy's black eyes.

"I think I see the motive behind it—" he began.

"If you do," said Van Cleef, "you're a damn fool. There's no motive. I'm talking to you as one human being to another. I thought that was what you wanted. But you can't take it. No. What you're looking for is reassurance. I haven't any to give. I don't know what life's all about. I can't tell you what you ought to do. I won't admonish you. I won't praise you. In fact, putting it frankly, I'm getting tired of talking about you."

The waiter set the broiled lobster before them; he glanced at Russell, but got not a word.

"I'm pretty sick of thinking about me," said Russell. "You're not afflicted like that. You don't think about yourself, do you?"

"No..." said Van Cleef, half to himself. "Can't. I'm a sort of ghost...."

He was tired, with the hopeless fatigue of a ghost. Nowhere to rest....

"If you'll keep on talking to me," said Russell. "If you can put up with me...."

He spoke humbly, miserably; he was asking most urgently for something most desperately needed. And Van Cleef, the ghost, refused no one. He admitted all claims. "Sure!" he said, and smiled.

II

"What's the street in Blackhaven?" Russell asked.

"Oh.... Big house, just off the Shore road. I'll tell you when to turn."

"Are you going to stay there long?"

"Couldn't say," Van Cleef answered, with resignation.

"Isn't it a week-end party?"

"Not a party. No. Y'see, the place used to belong to a friend of mine. Bill Swan. He died, two years ago, and his widow had this idea of running it as a boarding-house. Guesthouse, she calls it. Not a good idea."

"Look here! I might stay there, too," said Russell. "My car might be useful to you. I could run you anywhere you wanted."

"I never go anywhere," said Van Cleef, dismayed. "It's— there wouldn't be anything there for you. No young people."

"I'm not looking for 'young people'; I'd like to stay. Unless you don't want me."

"To tell you the truth," said Van Cleef, "this is what you might call a personal visit; see what I mean?"

"All right..." said Russell, with a faint smile.

"Well.... Damn you," thought Van Cleef, looking at him. "This won't do.... Altogether too sudden.... It's—what?—half-past two. Eleven o'clock this morning, this boy drops out of the sky. Doesn't live anywhere; hasn't any plans. Simply goes where I go. Won't do."

He was determined not to accept this preposterous responsibility. But he could, of course, be decent; he could be what the boy called a "human being."

"D'you like the country?" he asked.

"Oh, I love it!" said Russell. "The green grass and the blue sky, and the birds...."

This was heavy-handed irony; too clumsy to be annoying.

"He's a pest," thought Van Cleef. "But you've got to make allowances for his age.... Hilda was—let's see—twenty-three when she died.... Didn't seem so young to me then, because I was young, myself.... Next turn to the left!"

They turned off into a side road lined with fields, and before them rose Bill Swan's house; a long, flat-roofed rectangle of grey brick, faced with white, a two-tiered veranda with iron railing surrounding it, a little like a cage. The wide lawn before it was neglected; there were weeds in the drive-way; the house had somewhat the look of a child's creation, set down at random. Russell stopped the car before the door.

"Good-bye," he said.

"Come along in."

"You're tired of my company."

"Mistake, to talk like that," said Van Cleef. "Don't challenge people. Take it for granted that they're more or less agreeable. Come along in."

He pressed the bell, and promptly enough a coloured boy in a white jacket opened the door.

"How are you, Harly?" asked Van Cleef, seriously.

"Thank you, sir. Very well, sir," Harly answered, with equal seriousness. "I trust I see you well, sir?"

"Never better. Will you tell Mrs. Swan—" He stopped, at the sound of a step, and there she was, coming down the stairs, in all her incredible beauty.

She wore a black dress with a high collar and a little f, bow under one ear, incredibly chic, incredibly slight; her I lips had the half-petulant, half-wistful curves of a true Cupid's .'. bow; her brows were arched high above her heavy-lidded dark eyes; her curly dark hair was cut perfectly to the shape of her little head.

"Aa-rthur!" she said, stopping, with one delicate hand on | the banister rail.

"Hello, my dear girl!" he said; he smiled, but not she. "Emilia, this is Russell Blackman—"

"How *nice*!" she said.

She gave the boy both her hands, but, in spite of that I gesture, and her fervent tone, there was no warmth in her.

She looked at him, and it was obvious that she did not see him; some intense preoccupation made her lovely face blank.

"Do come in!" she said, and led the way across the wide, square hall, her high heels clicking prettily into a large square drawing-room furnished in a cold and conventionally handsome fashion. She sat down on a little Empire sofa, and her smoothly-fitting black dress fell into graceful folds.

The black bow under one ear gave her a coquettish look; the Cupid's bow mouth was formed in an eternal smile; only her eyes betrayed her.

"Will you ring, Aa-rthur?" she said. "We'll have tea."

"No, no. Don't bother."

"It's quite ready, Arthur. I'm sure Mr. Blackman...?"

Russell looked at Van Cleef, asking permission.

"Thanks," said Van Cleef.

There was a silence, which he made no attempt to break.

"No," he said to himself. "They're both too dramatic. I can't cope with 'em."

"I have only four people here now, Arthur," she said, at last. "Major Bramwell, and Annie and Harry Downes, and Lizzy Carroll-"

"I like Lizzy," he said.

"Oh, yes. They're all out now, except the Major. You won't mind if he joins us?"

"Why should I?"

Harly brought in a tea service and set it on a small table before the sofa; as he left the room, a man entered, a big man with short white hair and angry little blue eyes in a ruddy, heavy-jowled face. He stopped short, almost as if he dug his feet into the carpet, and stood straight as a ramrod, glaring.

"Carlo," said Emilia, "this is Mr. Van Cleef. Major Bramwell. And Mr. Blackman."

He gave a curt nod, and sat down on the sofa beside her.

"Another one," thought Van Cleef. "Poor girl."

She poured the tea and Russell became attentive, stood beside her, with an air of polite alertness. And she looked at him as she looked at any man, with the dainty smile of a Valentine.

"Because she can't help it," Van Cleef thought. "Doesn't mean anything. She's The Lady, and she treats us all as Gentlemen, which we aren't. She should have had a knight, poor girl, and what she got was Bill Swan, roaring around...."

The Major addressed himself to Russell.

"Well, young man!" he said. "Having a summer vacation?"

"Yes, sir," said Russell, in a modest tone.

"That your car out there? I suppose that's your idea of exercise—tearing around the country in a high-powered car."

"I'm very fond of walking," Russell said. "Only, it's hard to find anyone else who likes it."

"I wonder what *you* call 'walking,'" said the Major. "Four or five miles, along a smooth road."

"The best I ever did was twenty miles in one day, in Germany," said Russell, still modest, almost shy.

"Germany, eh?" said the Major. "Ever been in Switzerland? I had a curious experience there—"

"Arthur..." said Emilia. "I'd like to show you Regina's letter...."

The three men rose as she did, and Van Cleef followed her out into the square hall. She hesitated there, looking lost; then she led him to the dining-room. He lagged behind her, looking at the five small tables set up there, each with a white cloth and a little vase of flowers; he remembered how it had used to be in Bill Swan's day; the massive table, the sideboard with a fine display of silver....

Emilia looked back over her shoulder, and he moved to her side.

"Arthur," she said, "there's a horrible girl, trying to blackmail me."

"Sit down, and let's hear...."

She laid her hand on his arm.

"You're not taking it seriously! It's very serious for me, Arthur. This girl has somehow got hold of Annie Downes, and Annie invites her here—into my own house. It's—I can't tell Annie not to."

"D'you mean this girl has tried to get money from you, Emilia?"

"Not yet. But I know it's coming."

"See here, my dear girl.... Nothing she can blackmail you about."

"She can make up things."

"My dear girl!" he protested.

He had expected something wildly unreasonable; it wasn't possible to blackmail someone who had nothing at all. But this was sheer fantasy.

"Arthur, it's true!" she said.

"Sit down, Emilia."

"Arthur, she's putting ideas into Annie's head, horrible ideas—"

"Annie's told you?"

"No. But I can see."

He felt so tired. Tired of Emilia and her troubles. She had sent for him before and he always came, but the other troubles could be settled by a cheque; some bill that had grown like a snowball, a stern notice about taxes or assessments. The cheques were called loans; she wrote them down in one of her extraordinary books.... "When I get this place on its feet..." she always said, anxious and unhappy.

"She tries," he thought. "Does the best she can. It's too much for her, that's all."

He was ashamed to feel tired.

"Just put it plainly for me, my dear girl," he said. "I don't quite get it, d'you see? You say this girl's trying to blackmail you. Any—facts?"

She glanced at him, and then away.

"No," she answered. And that answer, unprecedentedly direct and simple coming from her, made an almost startling impression upon him.

"I think she's lying," he said to himself. "Not like her, to lie. She's truthful—too truthful for her own good, as a rule. Must be something here...." He spoke without looking at her.

"I might have a talk with Annie, find out what the girl's been saying—"

"Annie wouldn't tell you. She's very secretive. No.... I thought—if you could persuade the girl to go away...."

"Mean pay her something? No, my dear girl; that's a bad thing to start. If she's causing you any trouble, we'll find a way to stop it. What's her name?"

"Dulac," she answered. "Blanche Dulac. She works in that stationer's shop, opposite the railway station. Somehow she's scraped an acquaintance with Annie, and she's got Annie to bring her here to lunch. And—Annie's changed, very much."

"Still and all, my dear girl, that's hardly blackmail."

"No.... Perhaps it's not.... But I don't *like* her, Arthur! I don't want her here."

"Tell Annie—"

"That wouldn't do any good. You know how obstinate Annie is. Arthur, I don't *like* that girl!"

He lit a cigarette, still taking care not to look at her.

"Any definite reason for not liking her?"

And again she gave that answer—No!—that was so much too prompt and too clear, coming from her. Now he looked at her, and her dark eyes were unfathomable to him.

"It's really the change in Annie," she added. "And—it's something in the atmosphere... don't like to ask you to lend me any more, Arthur, but if that girl could be persuaded to go away—"

Her head was turned aside, so that the black bow was against the smooth curve of her pale cheek; her long lashes were down; she looked coquettish, charming, and completely baffling.

"That was how poor old Bill felt," he thought. "Damned artificial, he called her. It made him miserable, and so he made her miserable...."

"Aa-rthur..." she said, plaintively.

"Thinking things over, my dear girl," he said, hastily. "Give me a little more time, will you? They seem—complicated."

"Shall we go back now and have our tea?"

"Good idea!"

They were crossing the lounge, side by side, when Harly came, to summon Emilia to the telephone, and Van Cleef went on alone to the drawing-room. Russell was standing by the window, looking out; the Major sat by the tea-table, his hands on his knees; at sight of Van Cleef, he rose quickly, with a sort of quiver, like a spring uncoiling.

"I note that you have a bag with you, sir," he said. "If you contemplated an extended stay here, I have to tell you it is not convenient."

"Afraid I don't get you..." said Van Cleef, apologetically.

"I say it is *not convenient*, sir."

"Mean for me?"

"I do not. I mean it's not convenient for Mrs. Swan to—to receive you at this time."

"Oh, I see!" said Van Cleef, still apologetic. He struck a match for a cigarette and sat down on the sofa, his long legs stretched out, one hand in his trousers pocket.

"Do you intend to leave, sir, or do you not?" demanded the Major.

"Well, see here.... Let's not make an issue of it just now," Van Cleef suggested.

"You can't put me off this way, sir!" said the Major, and he was shouting now. "I ask you to leave this house immediately!"

"Perhaps you'd *better*, Arthur," murmured Emilia's voice at his side. "You could come back some other day...."

He rose politely, took his hand out of his pocket, and stood looking down at her.

"Well, no..." he said. "Sorry, but I think not."

There was a complete silence.

"Russell," said Van Cleef, "if you'll be good enough to drive me down to the village.... I'll leave my bag here, Emilia. I'll be back in good time for dinner."

He waited, but he got no answer; he smiled, vaguely, and went out of the room.

III

"I want a drink," said Van Cleef, simply, as he got into the car.

"All right. I'll keep an eye out for a bar," said Russell. "Which way is the village?"

"Left, along the boulevard."

"What d'you think of the Major?"

"Don't want to think of him at all," said Van Cleef.

"I wonder what it is he's so much afraid of...."

"Afraid?"

"It was pretty obvious, wasn't it? He wanted to get you out of the house—"

"Probably he didn't like me," said Van Cleef. "That can happen."

"He was panicked."

"I may even do that to people."

Russell turned the car into the wide, smooth boulevard.

"Something's going to, happen there," he said.

"Psychic?" asked Van Cleef.

The boy's dark face flushed.

"No. Just a half-baked young fool. Just a damn nuisance—"

"Y'know," said Van Cleef, "in a way, you are a damn nuisance, being so sensitive. If you feel like talking, talk. If you've noticed things, if you've got any ideas, go ahead."

Russell didn't answer for some time.

"Geoffrey Blackman is a second cousin of mine," he said, presently.

"Never heard of him."

"He's considered one of the leading psychologists in the country. In the world. He's let me do some studying with him, attend some of his clinics. He's interested in me."

"Well, there you are!" said Van Cleef, pleased. "Fellow's a prominent man, and he's interested in you. There's a career for you."

"The only trouble is, that he hates me."

"O God! I suppose you can't help being that way. Why d'you think he hates you?"

"He admits it," said Russell, smiling. "We've talked it over; we've analysed the situation. He's fifty, and he can't stand my being eighteen. He says he's going to watch my career with great interest, but he never wants to set eyes on me again."

"Must be plenty of other psychologists, if that's what interests you,"

"Criminal psychology. I'd like to be a super-detective, one of the scientific kind."

"I see! Nice work, if you can get it."

"Very nice work," Russell agreed. "It combines all the things that interest me—chemistry, medicine, psychology— and action."

"Hey! There's a bar!" said Van Cleef, and Russell backed the car, and turned into the drive before an imitation Swiss chalet. Incredibly loud music came out at them; a patron had dropped a coin into an apparatus that started a gramophone; the stamping beat of a rhumba filled the place.

"Straight Scotch," said Van Cleef to the waiter, and lit a cigarette, leaning back in his chair and watching Russell. The boy's fine dark brows twitched, his mouth tightened; he pushed back his chair.

"Sit down," said Van Cleef.

"I'm going to stop that damned filthy row—"

"Sit down! Can't be done. The fellow's paid his money; he has a right to his music."

Russell sat down, and the terrific music ended. But up got that client again, dropped in another coin, and this time it was worse; a monster voice bellowed the chorus of a song. Van Cleef finished his drink and rose; they got into the car again.

"If I ever make a fortune, or inherit one," said Russell, "I'm going to use the money to found an Anti-Music League."

"Mean Anti-Noise, don't you?"

"No. If you have money, you can keep away from noise. What I'd like to do, is to bar the mob, the canaille, from hearing music. I'd spend my fortune to keep Mozart off the radio. There'd be no gramophone records. I'd make it cost fifty dollars to hear an hour of Bach."

"Aristocratic," Van Cleef observed. "Ancient regime."

"How d'you know it's not new? It's possible that we've finished forever with the theory of democracy. It was never anything but a theory, and it grows more and more impossible as human breeding grows more chaotic. Superior men are becoming fewer, and they'll have to become more ruthless."

"Looking around the modern world," said Van Cleef, "the ruthless men don't seem biologically superior to me."

The boy glanced at him with a faint frown, and Van Cleef smiled broadly.

"What's so amusing?" Russell demanded.

"You underrate your fellow-creatures," Van Cleef answered. "Mustn't do that, when you become a super-sleuth. I'd like to see you, when you come up against the criminal Master-Mind."

"I'd like to come up against a criminal with intelligence, Russell said, thoughtfully. "I comb the daily news, looking for one, but I never find any."

"Some pretty slick financial crooks."

"That doesn't interest me. I don't think it's criminal to take money away from fools. There's only one crime that has colour and charm."

"Murder."

"Murder," Russell repeated. "To meet up with a really subtle murderer, to study him, catch up with him, step by step.... There can't be any other experience in life to equal a man-hunt."

"Poor devil!" thought Van Cleef. "I'm afraid his nastiness is genuine. Not a pose. May outgrow it, of course. But you can see why nobody likes him.... And the more nobody likes him, the nastier he grows.

Naturally.... Love thy neighbour as thyself.... But what if you don't love yourself?"

"This seems to be the village," said Russell.

"Right. Stop at that stationer's, will you? I'll be out in a minute. Or—tell you what. There's a liquor store around the corner. Might get me a couple of bottles of Scotch, will you?"

He got out of the car, in his headlong, lurching way, big shoulders stooped.

"We'll take a look at the blackmailing girl," he said to himself. "Very original idea, to blackmail someone who hasn't got a red cent...."

It was a very small shop, windowless; it would have been dark but for the setting sun that streamed in through the doorway and filled it with a dusty glory.

"Yes?" asked the girl behind the counter.

A young girl in a white dress. A slim girl with brown hair and grey eyes and a beautiful, generous mouth.

"What cigarettes do you recommend?" he asked.

"Well, I don't know..." she said, earnestly. "I guess it's a matter of taste."

"Suppose I haven't any taste?"

"Well, do you like Turkish or Virginia?"

"Have you any Havana cigarettes?"

"I'm sorry...."

"Any Russian?"

"I'm sorry. But there wouldn't be any demand for them in a little place like this." Suddenly she smiled, a grin so wide that it gave her the look of a kitten, all mouth and eyes. "I guess you come from New York," she said.

"Right! But how did you guess it?"

"I can almost always tell," she said, with a certain nonchalance. "Of course, lots of people stop in here; this street's a by-pass. I have a wonderful chance to study types. I bet that if I ever do get to New York—"

"Never been there?" he interrupted, surprised.

"Nope," she said, briefly.

"It's under two hours by train."

She said nothing to that. She was not smiling now; she looked almost stern.

"Anyhow," she said, after a moment, "it's not particularly important. I mean, you can learn just as much about life and human nature in a village as in a city. Look at the Brontes, for instance."

"Like to read?"

"Well, of course. Who doesn't?"

"I don't," he said. "I can't:"

Her clear eyes rested thoughtfully on his face.

"You're—" she began, and stopped suddenly, with a hot colour rising in her cheeks.

"I'm what? Please say whatever it was."

"No. It was—nothing."

"Y'know," he said, "I wander all over looking for someone to tell me what I am. Who I am."

"I couldn't tell you that," she said, with gentleness.

"You've got that feminine intuition," he said. "Nothing like it. You looked at me, and you got some sort of impression. It would help me, if you'd say it."

"I just thought—you weren't happy," she said.

He was curiously impressed, by the words and by the tone.

"Is anyone happy?" he asked.

"Lots of people."

"You?"

"I'm just beginning to be happy," she said. "I mean, when you're too young, you're waiting to be happy—waiting for life to begin. I'm just realizing that life isn't around the corner. It's now."

He took cigarettes out of his pocket and lit one, in an absent-minded way.

"I have an inferiority complex," he observed. "I think an inferiority complex is—a beautiful thing," said she, with a sort of vehemence. "I don't see why it's supposed to be wrong. It's—well—it means having a bumble and a contrite heart, doesn't it?"

He was silent for a long time.

"D'you mind—" he said. "Is your name—are you Mrs. Dulac?"

"Yes. Blanche Dulac. Why?"

"I'm paying a little visit at Mrs. Swan's—"

"Oh! Mrs. Swan!" she said, and the tone was unmistakable! She had no liking for Emilia.

"You re a friend of Mrs. Downes, aren't you?" he asked.

"Well, not exactly a friend," she said. "Mrs. Downes has been rather nice to me—in a way."

"She doesn't like Annie Downes, either," he thought.

"Thing is—" he began, when Russell entered the shop. He looked at the girl, and she looked at him, and it was, thought Van Cleef, the way two strange children look at each other, with curiosity, and interest, and faint hostility.

"Buying supplies?" asked Russell.

"I can't make up my mind," said Van Cleef.

"I've done your little errand for you...."

"Thanks."

There was a silence; Van Cleef leaned against the counter, smoking, gazing at nothing.

"Shall I go away, and come back in an hour or two?" asked Russell.

Van Cleef turned to the girl.

"I'd like a dozen packs of cigarettes, all different," he said.

She smiled at him, a different smile this time; there was a look of anxiety in her face. She wrapped up the package for him and handed it to him.

"I hope you'll come in again," she said, earnestly.

"Thank you," he said, taking off his hat. He kept it in his hand as he went out to the car.

"You're interested in women, aren't you?" said Russell.

"After all, such a lot of 'em around..." said Van Cleef. "It would be a bit hard not to notice 'em."

"But you like them."

"And you don't?"

"I don't."

"Unrequited love making you bitter?"

"I'm not bad-looking. I'm not stupid. And I have money. I could have a pretty wide choice—if I wanted."

"Sorry you don't smoke," said Van Cleef.

"Why?"

"If you did, maybe you wouldn't talk so much," said Van Cleef. He watched the dark flush that rose in the boy's face, saw the sullen thrust of his lip, and he was surprised by his own sense of satisfaction.

"Won't do," he thought. "This must be what happens to him all the time. He arouses in his fellow-creatures a passionate yearning to give him a kick in the pants. He knows it, and he can't help it. Kicks are very helpful, to some young people. Not to him. I don't want to, but maybe he's been sent by destiny.... Anyhow, here he is.... Thing is, I sit around with all the doors and windows open, and people get in. They don't know it's an empty house.... If you let them in, you've got to be affable...

He sighed, and looked at the sky for inspiration. The sun was going down, in a quiet and melancholy fashion; the car turned into the drive, and Emilia's house rose before them, neat and stark against the blank sky; the two-tiered balconies on each side looked, thought Van Cleef, like a cage supporting an unfinished structure.

"Are you going to defy the Major, and stay?" asked Russell.

"Oh—I think so...."

"He's a pathological case—"

"Aren't we all?"

"He's dangerous," said Russell.

"Don't agree with you."

"You're making a mistake," said Russell, curtly. "I wish you'd listen to me, and get away from here."

"What's the danger?" asked Van Cleef, with resignation.

"If I told you, you wouldn't believe me."

"No," said Van Cleef. "No.... I'm afraid I shouldn't."

"Then, if you don't object too much," said Russell, "I'll stay, too."

IV

He rang the bell, and the door was opened promptly by a grey-haired lady with a pince-nez.

"Arthur!" she exclaimed. "Emilia told me you'd come. I *thought* I heard a car...."

"Van Cleef!" said a man's voice behind her.

These were the Downeses. When he had first met them, or where, or how, Van Cleef had no recollection; he knew only that for fifteen years he had been meeting them—everywhere. He would go to a dinner party, and the Downeses would be there; they appeared at cocktail parties; they could be seen in restaurants, at plays; once he had met them in London, again in Paris, and it had been entirely natural.

"Maybe they're an hallucination," he thought. "Maybe nobody else sees them. I turn my head, and there they are."

They were, as always, extremely pleased to see him. Mrs. Downes had things to tell him about mutual friends.

"Have you heard," she said, "that Alicia is going to marry again?"

"The man's a cousin of Wellington, the writer," said Downes. "Were you with us when we met him in Paris, Van Cleef?"

"I don't know," Van Cleef answered, and that was true. "Maybe I was with them in Paris," he thought. "Or I wonder.... Is it "them," or "it"? Mean to say, are they actually two people, or different aspects of one Downes?"

Except for the fact that they both wore pince-nez, they were not physically alike. Harry Downes was a plump and elegant little man; Annie Downes was thin and untidy; the resemblance lay in their nebulousness.

"Woolly," thought Van Cleef. "Like clouds—or sheep."

They were not interesting; when he did not see them, he never thought of them, yet, for some reason, he was always pleased to see them.

"Are you stopping here long, Arthur?" Mrs. Downes asked, and he noticed that she was staring past him at Russell.

"This is Russell Blackman," he said.

"Blackman..." Mrs. Downes repeated, with an anxious frown. "Are you related to the Maryland Blackmans?"

"I don't know," said Russell.

"You don't know?" she said, taken aback. "But surely.... I met a Miss *Grace* Blackman in Egypt.... *She* was from Maryland."

"My people live in Boston," said Russell. "I don't know where they came from."

Nothing could have affronted Mrs. Downes more than this.

"That's very peculiar," she said.

"We know a good many people in Boston," said Mr. Downes.

"I don't," said Russell.

This was more than Annie Downes could endure. He was undermining the foundations of society.

"Very eccentric..." she said. "Tell me, Arthur, have you heard anything of the Telfairs lately? They seem to have disappeared off the face of the earth."

"I did hear a rumour—" Downes began, when Emilia entered.

"I've told Harly to make cocktails," she said, with her sweet Valentine's smile. "Do you want to go up to your room first, Arthur?"

He was silent for a moment.

"Can you put Russell up for the night?" he asked.

Because he felt sorry for the boy, standing there ignored.

"Oh, yes!" she said. "Harly will take up your bags—"

"I'm sorry, but I've come without anything," said Russell. "If there's time, I'll drive down to the village and get a toothbrush, and so on."

He spoke nicely to Emilia, and she smiled nicely at him.

"There's an hour before dinner," she said.

No one spoke until the boy had gone out of the room.

"Who is he, Arthur?" asked Mrs. Downes.

"I used to know his people. Very decent."

"I suppose," said Mrs. Downes, "that his rudeness is a pose. So many young people..."

"He's very handsome," said Emilia.

"Theatrical," said Mrs. Downes.

"Well!" said a new voice.

"My Lizzy!" said Van Cleef.

Miss Carroll held out both her hands, not smiling, looking at him with her cold blue eyes; a neat, spare little red-haired woman, pale, sharp-featured, supremely composed. Her fingers closed tightly on his big hands; then she let him go. Harly entered with a tray.

"Will you have a cocktail, Lizzy?" asked Emilia, ingratiatingly. "In honour of Arthur's visit?"

"I will not, thanks."

She lay down and took out a cigarette, and Van Cleef lit it for her. With an oddly youthful limberness she swung one knee over the other; very sporting, she looked, in a tailored blue silk blouse and a grey skirt.

"I've had a Mozart programme, for an hour and a half, on my radio," she said. "And that nonsensical Bramwell was bubbling around in his room all the time, muttering. He's insane."

"He doesn't like music," said Emilia.

"Then why does he stay in his room?"

"His work—"

"His work!" said Miss Carroll. "What does he think he's doing?"

"But he's told you, Lizzy. He's writing his reminiscences."

"Impossible. He's never done anything, and he's incapable of inventing anything."

"He has a medal," said Emilia, in her apologetic way, and Miss Carroll laughed.

"Change him to another room, my poor darling," she said. "Before one of us murders the other."

"If you're ready, Arthur...."

Van Cleef followed Emilia out of the room and up the stairs; as they reached the top, he leaned forward and took her hand.

"My dear girl.... I know a fellow who wants to buy a— a guest-house—"

"No, you don't, Arthur."

"If I can find someone to buy it—?"

She shook her head, and went on, holding his hand and drawing him after her. The room was familiar to Van Cleef; he had occupied it in Bill Swan's day; only now it was a little shabby, and a little dusty.

"I'll put that boy in the next room, and you can share the bath. Is that all right, Arthur?"

"That's all right, Emilia."

"You'll come down in a moment, for a cocktail, won't you, Arthur?"

"Oh, yes!" he said, and she left him.

He sat down in an arm-chair by the open window and lit a cigarette.

"A blackmailer?" he said to himself. "Not that girl. Honest, and gentle. Good. Good, without any complications. I wish I was good. And young. Or maybe I wish I were dead. That's possible—" He stretched, and sighed. "But probably I wish I had a drink," he thought. "What did my protege do with the whisky?"

It might still be in the car, in which case he couldn't very well go down and get it. He did not like cocktails; he did not want to join the group in the drawing-room. He closed his eyes, and went to sleep.

"Excuse me, sir. Excuse me, sir," said a soft and sorrowful voice from an immense distance, over and over again. "Excuse me, sir. Excuse *me*, sir—"

"My fault!" said Van Cleef, and opened his eyes. The room was dark; he couldn't see....

"Excuse *me*, sir...."

"Oh, Harly, is it? Yes?"

"The madam says, sir, shall she wait dinner for the young gentleman?"

"What young gentleman? Oh, yes.... No, don't wait. Turn on a light, will you, Harly? Thanks...."

The thin and melancholy Harly, soft-footed as a ghost, withdrew, and Van Cleef stepped out on to the balcony outside the window, to shake off his drowsy fatigue. At this side of the house the lawn sloped downward toward a coppice of young trees, and he saw something moving there. His sight was excellent; he moved forward toward the railing of the balcony; it was too low to lean over, but narrowing his eyes, he could see now that it Was a man moving among the trees; a small nimble man. He reached the wall that bordered the highway and climbed over it; there was a street light there, and for an instant it shone upon him, showed a dark face and a fierce white moustache, beneath a soft hat worn at a rakish angle. Then he vanished into the shadows.

"Very good conspirator," thought Van Cleef. "Is there something afoot here? Emilia and her talk about blackmail.... Major and his fury.... And now this little guy..."

He re-entered the room, to wash and get ready for dinner.

"Thing is," he thought, "Emilia makes things happen. She doesn't do anything. Things happen to her. She was on a ship that foundered. And there was Bill.... Drama...."

When he got downstairs, everyone was in the dining-room; the Downeses and Lizzy Carroll at one small table; the Major alone at another; Emilia sat at a table laid for three.

"Sorry to be late, Emilia."

"It doesn't matter, Arthur."

Each table had a vase of flowers and two green candles in silver holders; the china was fine Spode, but the plated ware was cheap and clumsy, and the cloth coarse. Harly, all alone, waited deftly upon everyone, setting before them the most minute servings of food.

"Emilia doesn't give a damn about eating!" Bill Swan had said once.

"Poetic," Van Cleef had suggested.

"Neurotic!" Swan had said. "It's unnatural. By God, you could give her a dish of that stuff—those dried roses— what d'you call it?—that potpourri, and she wouldn't care. She's not *human*."

"Poor old Bill..." thought Van Cleef. "You take a fellow like me.... I never did know what I wanted. Maybe I got it, and didn't recognize it. But Bill Swan knew exactly what he wanted, and he never could get it. He wanted to be a sort of feudal lord, benevolent, but supreme—"

"You're very quiet, Arthur."

"Sorry, my dear girl—"

"What happened to that boy?"

"I don't know. Quite natural for him to disappear. Came suddenly from nowhere, y'know."

"I like him," she said. "I wish I had a son as handsome as that."

"Lord!" thought Van Cleef, glancing at her charming face. "I suppose you're—you must be forty, or close to it. It's hard to believe...."

"*There* he is!" she said, and raised her hand, in a gay little salute to the boy who stood in the doorway. He crossed the room and sat down at the table with them.

"I'm sorry to be so late, but I couldn't find anything in the village, and I drove on, to Bainville."

Harly set a cup of bouillon before him, and presently took it away, untasted; brought a tiny ramekin of fish *au gratin*. Like Emilia, Russell seemed completely indifferent to food.

"Excited about something," thought Van Cleef. "What is there that could excite him, I wonder?"

The Major was the first to leave the dining-room, and he went directly upstairs. The Downeses went into the drawing-room; Miss Carroll went out on the veranda; and Van Cleef would have followed her, if Russell had not stopped him, with a hand on his arm.

"I've got something to tell you," he said. "Will you come upstairs?"

They entered Van Cleef's room, and Russell closed the door, and leaned against it.

"It was sheer luck," he said, his dark face alight. "I just happened to go into the chemist's in Bainville.... A woman came in and asked for a box of sleeping-tablets, one of the barbital preparations, and the chemist said he wouldn't give it to her without a doctor's prescription. After she'd gone I got talking to him. He told me that two years ago there'd been a death from an overdose of those same tablets, and he'd had to go into court and produce the prescription."

Van Cleef sat on the edge of a table, looking at the boy.

"The label he'd put on the box said, 'One as required,' and the coroner's jury gave a verdict of accidental death."

"Yes, I know."

"You know who it was—"

"Yes. Bill Swan."

"The chemist was very discreet but I gathered—"

"Yes," Van Cleef interrupted. "You gathered an earful of brutish gossip. I'm a friend of Emilia's. I was Bill Swan's friend. I heard all that. It's what happens in a tribe of savages. Everybody whispering 'poison—poison.'... Forget it."

"There's one aspect you may not have considered—"

"Forget it!" said Van Cleef, and there was no good humour in his face now. "And if you speak of it, or even hint of it again while you're under this roof, I'll take pleasure in kicking you out."

"You misunderstand me," said Russell, with a faint smile. "I didn't hear a word of suspicion against the person you're obviously defending."

"Then—" Van Cleef began, but thought better of it. "Forget it!" he said. "All of it." He rose and crossed the room; Russell moved aside to let him open the door, and he went slowly down the stairs. He found Emilia and Lizzy Carroll on the veranda, silent in the dark; he sat with them, smoking.

"I wonder if poor Emilia ever knew?" he thought. "Probably not. She was stunned by Bill's death—in a daze, for weeks. Wouldn't have noticed anything, and no one would have been likely to tell her. No. Probably never entered her head that any groups of friends were running around, saying of course they didn't believe poor dear Emilia had poisoned her dreadful husband."

It was a cool night, with a light wind that moved the white clouds across the starry sky; it was quiet, only insects chirping in the grass, and the trees rustling.

"I don't like peace and quiet," thought Van Cleef. "Makes me restless.... I'd like to have heard what that infernal Wonderchild was going to say, but it won't do to encourage him. Ever, in any way. Let the past bury its dead.... Everybody'd be glad to let it, if it would, only it doesn't.... That girl.... That Blanche.... I'll have to talk to Annie Downes about her. Set Emilia's mind at rest. That girl...."

That girl, who had spoken to him like a friend, yet was remote from him as if she lived in another era. She was beginning, opening a window upon a fresh, cool morning, and he was smothered with the dust of defeat. What had defeated him? He didn't know...."What's that?" he said, sitting forward.

Someone was running across the hall. The house door opened, and someone ran out, stood in the dark, breathing fast.

"Who is it?" cried Emilia.

They were all standing, waiting for an answer. And the answer came in Mrs. Downes's tremulous voice.

"Harry—doesn't feel well."

"Oh! I'm so sorry!" said Emilia. "Shall I call Doctor Robinson?"

"No.... Harry doesn't want a doctor. He thought—we thought—if Miss Carroll would just take a look at him—"

"Me?" said Miss Carroll. "*I'm* not a doctor."

"You're so—practical..." said Mrs. Downes.

"I'm certainly too practical to meddle with—" she began, but Mrs. Downes interrupted.

"Oh, do please hurry!" she cried, with a sob.

"Don't be hysterical!" said Miss Carroll. "I'll go and see Downes, but I can't do anything."

The door closed behind them.

"Aa-rthur.... Do you think I'd better go, too?"

"No," he answered, reassuringly. "They'll let you know if there's anything.... Probably nothing serious."

"Annie's changed so.... She's so hostile towards me.... I'm—" She paused. "Arthur.... Sometimes I'm *afraid* of Annie."

"My dear girl!" he protested.

"It's true! She's... There's something vindictive and dreadful about Annie Downes."

"Any definite examples?"

"Little things," she said. "Little things she's said and done. Ever since she first brought that hateful girl here."

He lit another cigarette.

"I stopped in to see the girl this afternoon," he said. "Didn't tell Her my name. Just wanted to see.... Emilia, you're wrong about her."

She said nothing to that.

"Only a kid," he went on. "Honest sort of kid."

"I asked you here to help me. I didn't—invent all this. Arthur, that girl will ruin me!"

"With gossip?" he said.

He heard her skirt rustle in the dark.

"There's something behind the gossip," she said, with a straightforwardness very unusual in her.

"Care to tell me?"

"No," she answered, and after a long silence, "I—sometimes I've felt quite sure—that you knew."

He wished now that he could see her face. Because her voice seemed unfamiliar; not the voice that belonged to the piquant and elegant little doll. It made him uneasy. More than uneasy....

"*You* knew—how things were," she said. "You knew how desperately unhappy Bill made me.... It was—too much...."

"My God!" he thought. "She can't mean... Shall I make her say plainly what she means? But if it's that... And if it's once said.... I don't know. I don't know whether it's better to let her go on, or not. It's—"

The door opened again, and closed smartly.

"That boy you brought, Arthur—" said Miss Carroll. "He's looking after Downes. He's giving him medicine—God know what—and Downes is swallowing it."

"What's wrong with him?" asked Van Cleef.

"Well..." she said, with deliberate hesitation, "he and his wife both call it indigestion."

"Not uncommon," said Van Cleef.

"If I had the sort of indigestion Downes has," said Miss Carroll, "I shouldn't be satisfied with a doctor. I'd call in the police."

V

They were perfectly silent and still there in the dark, all three of them.

"I'll go and see him," said Emilia.

"Don't," said Miss Carroll. "He's in pain. You won't like it, Emilia."

Their voices, disembodied in the darkness, were charged with infinite significance; it was as if they were moving stealthily around each other, looking for an opportunity for a rapier thrust.

"No..." said Van Cleef to himself. It was the protest of his body and his soul against an enormous responsibility; he was not adequate, he couldn't take charge. "I want a drink," he thought, aware of a familiar feeling, a sort of internal fluttering; the hand holding his cigarette was unsteady.

"If the man dies—" said Miss Carroll.

"Pull up your socks," Van Cleef told himself, and rose. "I'll go up..." he said. "Leave it to me, my dear girl."

"Arthur!"

"Leave it to me," he repeated, and groped for her hand, found it cold as ice. "Lizzy," he said, "better come along."

Miss Carroll entered the house with him; the light in the lounge dazzled him for a moment, so that she looked pale and fierce, her sandy hair had a coppery glint.

"No use upsetting the poor girl," he said.

"I'm sorry," said Miss Carroll. "Sometimes I forget that Emilia's peace of mind is the most important thing on earth. But Harry Downes doesn't forget it."

"What's the meaning of that, Lizzy?"

"I went in there," she said. "He was in agony. The only thing he said to me was, Tell Emilia not to worry!'"

"Humane."

"I hope Annie appreciates his humaneness," said she.

"I don't think I like women, Lizzy," he said, and turned towards the stairs. "Tempest in a teacup," he said to himself. "I hope to God it is."

The door of the Downes' room was open; he stopped on the threshold, profoundly disturbed by the scene. A small lamp on the bedside table cast a bright circle of light upon the figure of Downes, in vest and trousers, lying on his back with his eyes closed. Russell was bending over him, fingers on his wrist, a look of intense concentration on his fine dark face that made it noble. Annie Downes sat in a wicker armchair with her hands clasped in her lap; the light caught her glasses and made them glisten. It was not easy to break that silence.

"How is it going?" asked Van Cleef.

Russell, still bending over the prostrate figure, glanced up under his level black brows.

"I'm giving him a sedative," he said.

"D'you know what you're doing?"

"Yes. He'll be all right when he wakes."

Van Cleef came a few steps nearer, looking at Downes. Without his pince-nez, without a trace of his healthy colour, he looked strange. Very strange.

"We'll call a doctor," he said.

"It's not necessary," said Russell.

"Still and all, we'll have a doctor."

"No, we won't," said Annie Downes, in a flat voice. "If you call a doctor, I won't let him see Harry. You have no authority."

"Look here, Annie.... If anything—"

"If anything goes wrong, I'm responsible," she said, and rose. "I'm going to go to bed in one of the empty rooms."

"I'm sorry," said Russell, "but Mr. Downes can't be left alone.'

"Get someone else," said she. "I'm tired. I've got to rest. Good night!"

She went past Van Cleef, out of the room; her face had no expression except a sort of primness.

"You can't read faces," thought Van Cleef. "Some of 'em don't say anything..."

He turned again to Downes, whose face, very dreadfully, said nothing. "I'll now cut the Gordian knot, with common sense," he said aloud. "I'll get hold of a doctor—"

"You'd better have the facts first," said Russell, sitting down on the bed beside the motionless figure. "The man was poisoned with arsenic."

"Says you."

"All right. Get your doctor. Maybe it's an attempt at suicide, in which case they can arrest Downes. I've got the bottle here."

"What bottle?"

"Thermos bottle," said Russell. "It seems it's always left on the hall table downstairs, with a hot cereal drink for Downes. For his insomnia. He didn't take all of it."

"How the hell do you know there's arsenic in it?"

Russell got up, stood very straight and tense.

"I found this man suffering from arsenic poisoning," he said. "I found an empty cup beside him. I saved his life. Because I happen to know the symptoms, and the antidote."

"Happened to have the antidote handy?"

"Would you care to come into my room for a minute?"

"No, I don't think so."

"All right!" said Russell. "I've finished. Nothing more for me to do until I have to give my evidence in court."

"Why d'you want me to go to your room?"

"I have something to-show you."

"Can't leave this poor devil alone."

"It won't matter for ten minutes. We'll lock the door on the outside."

Van Cleef did that, and dropped the key into his pocket. They went along the corridor to a door at the end; Russell stepped in and switched on the light. A pleasant tranquil room, with a smooth white bed, and on the open flap of a little writing-desk lay a thin black kitten, stiff as a board, its teeth showing in a monstrous grin.

Van Cleef stood motionless, struggling against something horrible, against fury, was it, or nausea, or something else?

"What's the idea?" he asked.

"I was making an experiment," Russell answered, looking squarely at him.

"Killed this—little beast?"

"Yes. I wanted to make some observations."

Van Cleef turned his back on the boy, and lit a cigarette.

"Pack up your experiment, and what not, and get out, will you?" he said.

"All right!" Russell said. "You'd better listen to me first, though. Someone tried to murder Downes tonight, and someone succeeded in murdering Swap, two years ago."

"Pull yourself together!" thought Van Cleef. "This is serious. You can't just kick the boy out and forget it. Suppose he talks to somebody else?"

"I've covered up the 'experiment,'" said Russell, behind him. "Sorry I offended your finer feelings. Personally, I'm not sentimental about animals."

"Skip that. You were saying—"

"Do you want to hear? If you don't, we can skip all of it. I don't give one little damn about justice. To me this is an interesting problem, and nothing more. I'm willing to shut up about it, forever, if you like."

"I do want you to shut up," thought Van Cleef. "But that won't do." He sat down on the arm of a chair, still with his back to the desk. "Let's hear about all the murders," he said.

"This boy Harly was in the house when Swan died," said Russell. "I had a talk with him after dinner. He saw Swan an hour or so before he died, and he saw him ten minutes after he died. He remembers all the details."

"He gave his evidence at the inquest."

"Not about the cup."

"What cup?"

"The cup that wasn't there," said Russell.

Van Cleef drew on his cigarette, surprised, even alarmed, by the emotion that stirred him. For a long time he had taken his own equability for granted; he didn't get angry, or even irritated.

"I'll buy it," he said, presently. "Let's hear the Adventure of the Cup That Wasn't There."

"When I was talking to the chemist in Bainville, he said one thing that impressed me," Russell went on. "He happened to mention that Swan died at six in the evening."

"Is that an especially sinister time to die?"

"It's rather an unusual time to die from an overdose of sleeping medicine, isn't it?"

"I see your point. Go on."

"I got Harly talking."

"Cleverly, without arousing any suspicion in his mind, and so on?"

"You're right," said Russell. "I told him I'd gone to buy some sleeping medicine for myself, and that the chemist had told me Swan died from a dose of the same thing. I said I was nervous about taking the stuff now. I asked him if Swan had taken a hot drink with it."

"Why did you ask him that?"

"Random shot. I'd asked other questions that drew blank, but this one was good. He said that when he last saw Swan, there was an empty cup and saucer beside him. He was sure of it, because he wanted to take them away, and Swan said no. When he brought up the doctor, there was no cup."

"And you, and you alone were able to get this information out of him."

"No. He says he told the family lawyer."

"Ah-ha! So Perrson was in the conspiracy, too.... Perrson tell Harly not to mention the fatal cup?"

"The lawyer told him it was of no importance."

"But you know better."

"I'm sick of this!" cried Russell, with startling violence. "These people are friends of yours. I was doing this for you. And all you do is sneer at me.... My God! I believe you hate me!"

"I believe I do," thought Van Cleef, with a sense of shock.

He didn't like that, he didn't approve of hatred; he felt unhappy, and wholly confused. He was silent, staring at the floor for a time; then he looked up at the boy with an uneasy smile.

"Sorry!" he said.

"For what?"

"Hell!" said Van Cleef with a sigh. "I dunno.... Anyhow, suppose we drop the sleuthing?"

"You want me to drop it?" Russell asked, looking at him with narrowed eyes and a faint smile. "Now? After what's happened to Downes?"

"Better be getting back to Downes now.... We can see what he has to say when he recovers. Mean to say, if *he's* satisfied..."

"Ah right!" said Russell. "It's up to you."

He went past Van Cleef, out of the room, without another word, or a glance.

"I need a drink," thought Van Cleef. As he rose, he was obliged to glance towards the desk where the kitten lay, covered with a clean white linen handkerchief. "I need a drink. I don't like this—any of this."

He went into the hall towards his own room, wanting a drink very badly. Quite suddenly the boy's last words came back to him. "It's up to you."

"Up to me?" he asked himself. "Can't see it."

Two bottles of Scotch stood on the chest of drawers. He opened one of them.

"Thing is, if it's up to me.... Better keep a clear head...."

He didn't take a drink. He went out into the hall again, and he saw Lizzy Carroll sitting in Downes's room, wearing a flannel dressing-gown, and reading a book. She glanced up at the sound of his step, and looked at him sharply and sternly. With reluctance he went down the stairs in search of Emilia, to give her what reassurance he could. He did not find her in the house, and he thought, with another sigh, that she might still be on the veranda, alone, in the dark, thinking—Heaven knew what. He opened the house door.

"Get rid of the man!" Major Bramwell was saying, in a high, unsteady voice. "I tell you, Emilia, he's dangerous! He's an irresponsible—sot."

Van Cleef closed the door softly and went directly upstairs, and poured himself a drink.

"Sot, is it?" he said to himself. "Unpleasant word...."

He hated the smell of whisky, hated the taste of it; the first sip made him shudder. But it helped. Pulled him together, cleared his mind. When he had swallowed that drink, he sighed, leaned back, relaxed, lit a cigarette.

"I'm committing the supreme psychological sin," he thought. "Refusing to face facts. I don't like Russell's notions, therefore I refuse to consider them. Won't do. I'm alone now. I don't have to be on the defensive. How does the set-up really look? Downes is taken sick. That's a fact. Lizzy Carroll thinks it queer. That's not a fact; that's a notion. Russell says it's arsenic, and that he's got a sample of it. That may be a fact, or it may be a notion. It ought to be tested, anyhow."

He poured out another drink.

"Anyhow," he repeated to himself. "Nothing so bad as rumour, gossip. I don't know whether Emilia ever knew what people were whispering, two years ago.... But here it is, cropping up again.... All right! By God, I *know* she didn't poison Bill! How do I know it? How does anyone know that his friends aren't assassins, thieves, blackguards? I've seen her, observed her for eight years. She's not a murderer. The poisoning of Bill Swan is very definitely a notion of Russell's. No evidence then, and no evidence now. *If* Downes has been poisoned, it's an isolated incident. Nothing to do with Bill Swan. Who'd want to poison Downes? Nobody. Who could have poisoned him? Anybody. The thermos bottle was on the table in the hall. Anybody could have put arsenic into it. What is arsenic? A powder? A pill? A liquid? Can anybody buy it? Russell bought some sort of poison. That little cad...."

He swallowed the rest of the drink, and put away the bottle.

"When you come to think of it, that's a damn queer coincidence.... Russell went out before dinner, in his light-hearted, boyish way, to buy a spot of poison. And after dinner, Downes got a dose. Maybe Downes was just another experiment.... Russell's story is, that he saved Downes's life. He doesn't impress me as the life-saving type. I'm prejudiced. I admit it. I think Russell's probably Satan. All right! How can I find out? How can I find out anything, about anything? Go to the police? With what? Downes and his missus won't back me up. They wouldn't have a doctor. *That's* queer. Does it mean suicide? This bores me. Like the way those detective johnnies in books recapitulate. They do it aloud, though, with a Watson to check up. They use numbers, or letters. Or both. One—A: Has anything really happened at all? One—B: If so, what? Two—A: If not, why not, and who is responsible?"

He rose and stood looking out of the window, and suddenly he remembered the man with the white moustache.

"Who the hell was that?" he thought. "He was certainly what they call skulking, or prowling... May have been simply an outside burglar. Thrown in to make things harder. Or—"

Something else came back to him.

"I'd forgotten what brought me here. Emilia's blackmail case.... I'd forgotten-that girl.... That Blanche...."

Sorrow came over him in an overwhelming tide; a dreadful sense of loss. He brought the bottle of whisky back to the table and opened it again.

"Such an honest kid.... So kind.... 'I just thought you weren't happy,'... You're right, my dear little kid. Not happy.... Sots aren't—very happy...."

VI

It was early when Van Cleef awoke; he never slept long. He got up immediately, as was his habit, filled with a familiar restlessness. He went into the bathroom and took a cold shower; he had just stepped out of the tub, when the other door opened, and Russell stood there, in shirt and trousers, bare-foot, his black hair disordered, his eyes heavy.

"I'm sorry," he said, sombrely.

"All right!"

"I was a bit beyond myself," Russell went on. "But I'd had a shot of morphine."

"What?"

"Oh, I'm not an addict, if that's what you're thinking," said Russell, with a frown. "I don't take the stuff once in six months. I needed it yesterday."

"Sick?"

"I've never been ill in my life. It's something else. It's a depression—a feeling of inadequacy and failure.... Maybe you can understand."

Their eyes met for an instant; Van Cleef looked away, went on dicing himself with a flimsy Turkish towel.

"Can't be anything but a random shot," he thought. "Boy can't know how I feel...."

He stretched out the towel, to dry his broad shoulders, and it came in two; he looked at it in surprise.

"I didn't kill the cat," said Russell.

"You said it was an experiment."

"I found it in the road, run over. I brought it in and gave it a morphia injection."

"How about the rest of it? About saving Downes's life?"

"That stands."

"Very interesting. Very curious. I mean your having antidotes all ready."

"I didn't. I found what I needed in Downes's own room. He has two shelves in a closet, packed solid with drugs. Either he or his wife must be a first-class hypochondriac."

"So, in the end we have this. That Downes had a stomachache and you gave him something, and he got over it."

"Downes was poisoned," said Russell.

"If he doesn't mind, or his wife doesn't mind... Going to get dressed now."

Van Cleef went back into his own room, closing the bathroom door on Russell.

"Pleased to hear he didn't kill the little beast," he said to himself. "But still and all... You get the impression that he would do things like that...."

He dressed with care, as he always did; he paid fabulous sums for his suits, his shoes, for everything; he was fastidious to the point of fussiness. Not from vanity; it was an article in his queer, confused code, that a man must look decent. When he was ready, he went downstairs, and into the dining-room, and he was glad to see no one there except Miss Carroll.

"How's my Lizzy?" he asked.

"I don't know, Arthur. I sat up with that idiot Downes all night. I suppose I dozed in my chair, but it didn't seem that way."

"How's he doing?"

"He slept all night, and he seems perfectly well this morning. Annie's making some sort of hot drink for him. Arthur—I don't like it!"

He sat down at the table opposite her, and Harly came to his side.

"What would you wish, sir?"

"Oh... Coffee..." he answered. "Just coffee, thanks...." He waited until the boy had gone. "You're tired, Lizzy."

"Arthur," she said, and her tart voice had an undertone of sadness, "you'd like to turn life off, like a tap. Make it stop. It worries you to hear it keep on running. But it doesn't stop. There's no use pretending there's nothing wrong here. You can run away from it, if you like, of course—"

"What's wrong, then?"

"Emilia," she said. "Poor darling! She's a femme fatale, without even knowing it. It's rather like seeing a child with a machinegun; not a very bright child, either.... That idiot Downes was talking about her in his sleep.... 'You can trust me, Emilia.... I'll never tell. You can trust me never to tell any one!'

Van Cleef frowned miserably.

"What would that mean, d'you think?"

"I've no idea. But if he has a secret, Annie certainly knows. Knows, I mean, that he's concealing something. She's been married to him for some thirty years. If he's infatuated with Emilia, Annie must know it. And it couldn't please her much."

"Let's have everything in words of one syllable. All plain."

"I think Annie poisoned him," she said.

"My dear girl!"

"That's what I think. And I think he'd have died, if your Russell hadn't been so clever."

Harly brought a cup and saucer, and a pot of coffee; he waited a moment, and then withdrew.

"It's hard," said Van Cleef. "Extraordinarily hard to see Annie Downes in that light."

"Not at all. She's fading. Growing old; she hasn't a penny of her own; she has nothing, no position, no occupation except her husband. If she saw—or thought she saw him turning to another, younger woman—"

"Logical thing would be to try and remove the woman."

"Maybe she will," said Miss Carroll.

"Mean you think—there's more to come?"

She was silent for a time. She was neat as a pin, in a fresh white shirt and a tweed skirt, her red hair in a smooth knot; her pale, sharp-featured face was composed, but there was some shadow upon it....

"I had premonitions, last night," she said, presently. "I don't believe in them—but at the same time, I do believe in them. Especially at four o'clock in the morning."

"Premonitions of what?"

"Just horror, Arthur."

"All right!" he said. "Let's break the spell—bust up the whole thing. You help me. We'll get Emilia to give up the guest-house—persuade her to take a trip—"

"Good morning!" said Bramwell's voice, beside them. "Boy!" he shouted, and Harly came running.

"I'll back you up, Arthur, to the best of my ability," said Miss Carroll, "but-"

The rest of the words were drowned by the Major's bellow.

"Damn you, boy! Trying to be impudent?"

"No, sir!" said Harly, in extreme distress.

"You are impudent! You know damn well that I don't eat this muck—"

"Don't make such a noise," said Miss Carroll. "Can't you go outdoors to have your fits?"

He rose, and he was shaking, his blue eyes blazing.

"Madam!"

"Sir!" said Miss Carroll, unperturbed. "You're being ridiculous."

"I'm being persecuted!" he said. "But I know how to defend myself, and I intend to do it!"

Russell slipped quietly into the chair beside Van Cleef; at sight of him, the Major fell silent, and in a moment sat down again.

"What will you have, sir?" the anxious Harly ask Russell.

"Everything you've got," said Russell. "I'm hungry."

"That's right!" said Miss Carroll, with an air of indulgence that surprised Van Cleef. "Did you go in to see Downes? How was his pulse?"

Russell answered; she asked more questions. They were serious, friendly, professional, like a doctor and a nurse. It was extraordinary, thought Van Cleef, and rather touching, the way the boy responded to her amiability. Perhaps it was something more than touching, to be alight with pleasure for so small a benefaction....

Emilia came into the room, and the Major, Van Cleef and Russell all rose.

"Oh, please sit down!" she said, earnestly. "I just came to see if everything was quite all right?"

Her dark hair grew in a point on her forehead; what they call a widow's peak, he thought; her dark brows were so arched as to look artificial. It suited her, to look artificial. She was wearing a black skirt, and a ruffled white blouse; she was a charming imitation of a boarding-house mistress, with boarders who rose as she entered.

"What's real in her?" he thought. "Does she love anyone, or hate anyone? Is she happy, or unhappy?"

She smiled at him, looking straight into his eyes, as if there were no one else. She always had done that to him, to Bill, to everyone. Maybe she didn't realize how fervent a look it was; and maybe she did.

"When you've finished, Aa-rthur," she said, "would you like to look at the flowers?"

"Finished now," he said. "If you'll excuse me, Lizzy...."

He followed Emilia across the hall, and through the drawing-room to what Bill had called "the conservatory"; it was little more than a large bay-window, shut off by glass doors covered by curtains. He hated to look at the place now. Bill had had a gardener, and a rather ostentatious collection of brilliant flowers, but now it was lamentable, pots of earth dried into dust, with stalks standing up in them, dead dry vines nailed against the walls; the spring sun was dimmed by the dusty windows, the air smelt of dust.

"There..." she said, resting her delicate hand on the edge of a wooden box where three pansies were still alive. "They're quite sweet, aren't they?"

"Oh, very!" he said, and waited.

"Arthur..." she said, "*now* you know what I mean, don't you?"

"Sorry, my dear girl..." he protested, anxiously.

"Oh, Arthur! Surely you see now what that girl has done?"

"No. Sorry, but I can't."

"She's set Annie against me so completely.... She's put this horrible, absurd idea into Annie's head." She paused, touching the velvety petal of a pansy with her forefinger. "This idea of poison," she said in a low tone, her eyes downcast. "For that to come up *again*.... It's too much...."

"Nothing's come up, my dear girl."

"If you could make her go away, Arthur!" she cried. "If you'd only believe me, that *she's* the cause of all this...."

"Emilia, look at it reasonably, my dear girl. What motive could she have for trying to stir up trouble? Thing is, you're tired, and a bit overwrought. No, listen, please! I'm sure this fellow I spoke about would buy the house—"

"You, too?" she said, still with her eyes downcast. "This is my home. You agree that I've got to go—to be driven out by the cruelest slander?" At last she looked up at him, "This is my home. I love it. *Must* I be driven out—by Blanche?"

"Not by Blanche. Couldn't be. There's no sense in it."

"I wish she was dead!"

That cry was the more shocking because her face didn't change, that heart-shaped Valentine face with the arched brows, with Cupid's bow mouth.

"You don't wish that, Emilia," Van Cleef said, briefly.

"No. Of course not," said she, turning away. "I only wish she'd live somewhere else...."

"Last night you said—you mentioned—that there was— something behind this gossip.... We're old friends. Mean to say, perhaps if we talked more frankly—"

"There's vindictiveness behind it," said she. "That's all. Malice and vindictiveness. Not one word of truth." She opened the glass door into the drawing-room. "But people can be destroyed by lies," she said, and went out.

Van Cleef looked at his watch.

"Too early..." he said to himself. Because he had a rule: no drink before eleven. He couldn't remember when he had adopted the rule, or why, but it was somehow of great importance. He had nearly two hours to wait, two hours of this vague restlessness. He went upstairs to the open door of the Downes' room, and it was, for some reason, a relief to see Mrs. Downes in there, knitting.

"How's the patient?" he asked.

"I'm better, thanks, Van Cleef," Downes answered gravely, "but I'm still shaky. I'll have to be careful, very careful of my diet, for some time to come."

"Any sinister meaning?" thought Van Cleef.

Downes did not look sinister, or even very ill; his face was a little sallow, but he lay back on a mound of pillows with a comfortable air.

"I have a nervous stomach," he continued. "In a way, that's bad, but in another way it is good. My digestion is very easily upset, but, on the other hand, sufficient rest will almost always restore it."

Quietly and earnestly he described his digestive processes, as they seemed to him.

"Harry had an attack exactly like this when we were in Cairo," said Mrs. Downes. "The doctor there—he was a Pole—a wonderful man... he said—"

Leaning against the doorway Van Cleef kept an attentive expression, without listening to a word.

"Cosy scene," he thought. "Leave well enough alone? Question is... Too damn many questions—and who am I, to answer them? Only one definite idea in the brain; to wit, that Blanche is not a scandalmonger, not vindictive, not anything but a nice lad. *She* could be talked to. She alone."

For half an hour he displayed a vaguely polite interest in Downes's digestion, and then he crossed the hall to his own room. Harly was dusting the lampshade; the bed was made, everything in order.

"Housemaid gone?"

"Yes, sir. Just me left, sir."

Van Cleef closed the door, and poured himself a drink.

"Only ten o'clock," he thought. "This is the beginning of the end. A sot.... Well..." He swallowed the drink, and recorked the bottle; he went in search of Russell, and found him in his bedroom sitting at a desk and writing. "Busy?"

"Nothing important," Russell answered, with a sidelong glance.

"Wants to be asked," thought Van Cleef, and did ask, "A spot of science?"

"No. I was making a psychological analysis of the people in the house for my own amusement."

"Too much!" said Van Cleef, half to himself. "Well, the thing is, if you can spare the time, want to drive me to the village?"

Russell answered fluently in a foreign language.

"Meaning *con amore*?" said Van Cleef, with a sigh. "All right, let's go."

It was good, he thought, to get away from that house; he lit a cigarette and slouched down in the roadster.

"Where do you want to go?" the boy asked.

"Stationer's."

"She's a pretty girl," said Russell, with a half-smile. "I wish you luck."

"Let it go!" Van Cleef told himself. "He's like that, and forever will be."

The main street was busy this morning, cheerful in the clear sun. Russell stopped the car at a corner.

"Shall I wait?" he asked. "Or come back?"

"Neither," said Van Cleef. "Thanks for the buggy ride, and adieu."

A young fellow in overalls was leaning on the counter, talking to Blanche, both speaking quietly, earnestly. Van Cleef stood unnoticed just inside the doorway of the dim little shop.

"Well, so long, Babe!" said the young man, presently. "Be seeing you!"

"Be seeing you!" she answered absently, and stared after him with a small frown. When Van Cleef came into her line of vision, she looked at him in the same way, not surprised, not pleased; simply accepting him. "Hello!" she said.

He liked that reception more than anything; it seemed to him more friendly than a smile, more welcoming than a handclasp. "Hello!" he answered. "I was wondering—" He moved away as someone else entered, stood inspecting the three shelves of books beneath a sign, "Lending Library,' until behind him he heard a fierce, hissing whisper in French.

"How much hast thou received?"

"Rien," answered Blanche, nonchalantly. "*C'est tout-a-fait fini, ca.*"

Van Cleef wanted a look at the customer, he turned his head. He saw a short man with a fierce white moustache, and a somewhat theatrical wide-brimmed, black felt hat. It was the man he had seen moving among the trees last night. There was no more conversation; the man with the moustache went briskly out of the shop, with a straight and soldierly bearing.

"Rather unusual type," said Van Cleef.

"That's my father," she said.

"French?"

"He was born in France, but he's lived here for ages. He's a night-watchman at the hat factory."

He lit a cigarette and stared at it.

"Emilia asked me to look into this," he thought. "That's why I'm here. Emilia says this girl is making trouble for her, and I've been denying it. Why? Because I like her. I like her so well that I'm not afraid to ask questions."

"Would you like to sit down?" she asked.

"Thing is, can you get out of here?"

"Well, how do you mean?" she asked.

"Could we take a walk or a drive?"

"You mean now?" she asked. "Right now?"

"That was the idea."

She thought it over for a moment.

"I guess so," she said. "If I can get hold of Mrs. Klein."

She was accepting this, too, without comment; she disappeared through a door in the back of the shop and he heard her running upstairs; she was down again, promptly.

"It's all right," she said. "I can have an hour."

They walked out of the shop; that was all there was to it.

"Is Mrs. Klein the boss?" he asked.

"Boss's wife."

"Are they nice to work for?"

"Yes," she said. "But, you see, I started in the right way. I told Mr. Klein, before I took the job, that I wanted to be a human being. I said I was willing to accept a nine-hour day, but that if I wanted to take time off, I could do it, and make it up another time. And without giving any reasons, either. I specially said that. Sometimes I haven't any reason; I mean, not a reason I could explain. I just feel like—not going to work."

"Not a very interesting job, is it?"

"No, it's not," she admitted. "Would you like to see the nice houses? If you do, we turn left here."

"Don't care too much for the nice houses, do you? My idea was, we might take a taxi, and go somewhere for lunch."

"It's pretty early..." she paused. "Thanks! I'd like that."

They crossed the street to the railway station, and got into a taxi.

"Is there a restaurant?" he asked.

"Well, there's Franchi's," she said. "They say the food is good, but it's sort of disreputable."

"Any other place?"

"I'd *like* to go to Franchi's," she said, "if *you* don't mind."

"Maybe your father wouldn't like it."

"He never interferes with me," she said. "He's brought me up to be independent. That's one of his theories."

She leaned back in the corner of the cab, looking out of the window, and Van Cleef looked at her; at her straight little nose, her short upper lip, and the quiet vigour there was about her. Clear features, clear skin, clear voice; all definite, he thought.... Then she turned her head, and her grey eyes had that look of gentleness again.

"Mr. Van Cleef.... If you've got something on your mind.... If there's anything I can do...."

He felt a sudden sharp desire to be definite, himself. But he could not be. There was an unhappy confusion in his mind about Emilia; there was his confirmed habit of vagueness. For so long a time he had managed not to judge, not to criticize, not to care; for too long a time. Blanche was waiting for an answer, and he could not give one.

"I need a drink," he thought.

"Is it something about Mrs. Swan?" she asked.

He looked at her, and a sort of anguish filled him; because he could not answer, could not be honest and clear.

"I need a drink," he said aloud.

He saw her eyes fill with tears, and he was amazed.

"Sorry..." he said.

She smiled, uncertainly, and turned away her head, looked out of the window; they said nothing more until they reached the sort of disreputable Franchi's, a road-house like a hundred others.

"Might wait," he said to the taxi driver.

They mounted the steps to the glass-enclosed veranda; no one there, nothing ready, chairs were piled one upon another; a swarthy man with a black moustache came hastening out, with an anxious deference. The menu, he said, was not quite ready, but they could have anything, anything they wished, chicken.... Very nice chickens....

"Cocktail?" Van Cleef asked the girl.

"Yes, thanks!" she answered.

"What kind?"

"I don't care," she said. He ordered a Martini for her, and a Scotch for himself; they sat down at a table and waited; a waiter came and spread a cloth on it, brought the drinks. She took a sip of hers and set it down.

"Mr. Van Cleef.... Is there anything you want to ask me?"

He swallowed his drink, and held up his glass to show the waiter.

"It's hard to get at..." he said. "Emilia—Mrs. Swan, y'know.... Feel like telling me your point of view about her?"

"I don't know what I think—now," she said. "I've been trying to make up my mind.... Before I'd met her, I believed what I'd heard, but now I don't know...

There was a pause.

"What had you heard?" he asked.

"My father says she's a murderess," said Blanche.

VII

It was a shock to hear that word, and it was a relief.

"Dangerous thing to say," he observed.

"He's never said it to anyone but me. He came home one day, and asked me to take a walk. There was something so queer about him.... We went past the Swans' house, just as Mr. Swan's funeral was coming out. Father stood here with his hat off. Mrs. Swan came by in a car, all in black with a veil over her face, and Father said: That woman is a murderess.' I didn't say anything then; I couldn't. But a few days later I asked him about it; I asked him if he was sure. And he said yes. I asked him why he didn't tell the police, and he said: 'It's too late. They couldn't do anything. But she'll pay for it, in the end.'"

"You're a bit matter-of-fact about it," said Van Cleef.

"I try to be," she said. "I can't tell you how I hate anything—melodramatic. I want to be—" She paused. "I want to be quiet about things."

"Yes..." he said.

"You see," she went on, "I've been brought up in a sort of melodrama. Father's the most upright, honourable man; he is very kind, and generous to people, really, but his ideas are so—so violent. Ever since I can remember, he's been talking about a class war, about enemies, about the day of reckoning. He sent me to a queer little school where we heard that sort of talk all the time. I never liked it. I don't want to hate anyone. I couldn't hate Mrs. Swan."

"Do you think your father hates her?"

"I know he does. He said so."

The waiter brought the fried chicken, excellently cooked, but he felt no appetite.

"You don't?" he said. "You've been seeing a lot of her, lately.... Been visiting Annie Downes...."

"I'm glad to be able to talk about this," she said, slowly. "It's been worrying me—" She raised her eyes to his face. "It's—queer!" she said. "I don't understand it. I don't like it."

"How did it begin?"

"Mrs. Downes came into the shop one day to buy a magazine, and got talking. She seemed—just friendly. When she asked me to come and see her, I was glad to go. I was curious to see Mrs. Swan. And I'd never been in a house like that. But when I got there... I didn't like it."

"Any special reason?"

"I guess there's always a reason for those—feelings," she said, soberly. "Even if you're not conscious of it. I've tried to think it out, but I haven't grasped it yet."

"What sort of 'feeling'?"

She considered that, and he watched her with an indefinable pleasure, a sort of delight in that sobriety. She wanted to say exactly what she meant.

"I think Mrs. Downes is using me for something," she said. "I've been there three times, but I'm not going again."

"What does she talk about?"

"Nothing. Just about knitting, or books or things like that."

"You can't think of anything out of the way that she's ever said?"

"There's never been anything. We just sit there, in the drawing-room and—chat, that's the word for it. Once I had lunch with her and Mr. Downes, and he was queerer than she. He didn't talk at all."

The waiter brought two little biscuit tortonis.

"I love this!" she said. "But what time is it, Mr. Van Cleef? Twelve-fifteen? I'm sorry, but I'll have to get back."

"Didn't like your cocktail?" he asked.

"No, thank you," she said, and he saw a faint colour rise in her cheeks.

They got back into the taxi again, set off towards the village.

"Shan't see her again," thought Van Cleef. "No reason for seeing her. She's not conspiring against Emilia. She's all right. How do I know? I do know. I'd go into court and swear.... This is a good and honest child."

He got out with her in front of the shop.

"Good-bye," he said. "And thanks."

"I'll see you again, won't I?"

"Oh, sure to!" he said.

There was something on her mind; he could see that; she stood in the sunny street, her eyes downcast. Presently, she looked up at him.

"Mr. Van Cleef!" she said. "I—won't you *please*—look after your health?"

"What?" he said, startled. Then he understood her. "I see..." he said. "Thanks, dear."

On the way back to the house, he thought about that.

"Means alcohol," he thought. "Take care of my 'health,' so I can go on and on—nowhere.... No. Something's broken. Mainspring?"

They were still at lunch when he entered the house, and he went quickly and quietly up to his own room.

"Something wrong about Annie Downes," he thought. "Blanche felt it. Well, suppose she did try to poison Harry? Where do we go from here? And Papa Dulac calls Emilia a murderess.... And Lizzy Carroll thinks it was a case for the police. And Russell 'knows.' Russell knows everything. I have only one idea, but it is a sound one. Emilia's got to give up this place, go somewhere else. Annie and Harry can settle their differences elsewhere...."

He stayed shut in his room, because he did not want to talk. But he had nothing to read, nothing to do; he walked up and down, smoking, thinking; and disgusted, bored with his thoughts.

"What was Papa Dulac doing here? Emilia's afraid of Blanche. Why? Maybe no reason. She's not a reasonable creature.... Downes.... Maybe he doesn't think he's been poisoned, or maybe he doesn't mind. Or maybe he's afraid to mention it."

There was a knock at the door.

"It's Russell!"

"This is my silent hour," said Van Cleef. "Meditating."

"I'd like to speak to you."

"I'll have to resist the temptation."

"It's important"

Van Cleef opened the door, and the boy entered.

"I've had that cereal drink analysed," he said. "There was arsenic in it."

"You have a one-track mind."

Russell stood looking straight at him.

"Of course," he said, "if you don't want this cleared up, that's all right with me. I don't give a damn whether or not all these people poison one another. I'll drop it if you like. I thought that very likely you had all the fine old traditions of justice, and truth, and so on."

"Drop it!" said Van Cleef. "Find another diversion, more suitable to your age. There's a Country Club here. Emilia's a member. Tell her you'd like to play tennis there this afternoon."

"What about going back to New York?"

"Good idea!" said Van Cleef. "Nothing much here for you."

"I mean, going together."

"No. I can't, just now."

"You prefer to stay here until there's another attempt at murder? Possibly successful the next time."

"Yes," said Van Cleef, with a great sigh.

"You won't take it seriously?"

"I won't take it at all," said Van Cleef. "Rather leave it. There's nothing to worry about, and anyhow, I'm not good at worrying. Let me have peace."

"You've come to the wrong place for 'peace,'" said Russell, and went out.

Later in the afternoon, Van Cleef was obliged to agree with that. A door was opened, and slammed shut; someone was knocking; he looked out, and it was

Major Bramwell, knocking at a door across the hall. Lizzy Carroll opened it.

"May I request you, madam," he said, "to—*move* that radio?"

"Don't bother me!" she said. "I've just got a very good programme—"

"You-your instrument is placed directly against the wall of my room, causing a—vibration—"

"Change your room. Emilia suggested it—"

"I won't!" he cried. "I won't! I came here first—"

"You're unbelievably childish," she said, looking at him in a sort of scornful wonder. "And you're a nuisance. I'm going back to listen to my programme, and if you knock on the wall again, you'll be sorry."

"You're—you're insane!" he cried. "You take an insane pleasure in tormenting people. I know very well who's responsible for the persecution I've been subjected to. Persecution—"

Miss Carroll retired into her room and closed the door; he stood there, scarlet with rage.

"Might take a walk..." Van Cleef suggested. "Exercise—"

"You're insolent, sir!"

He came nearer to Van Cleef, his blue eyes glaring. And with a sigh, Van Cleef, too, closed his door.

"Don't like quarrels," he said to himself.

After a few moments, he went in search of Emilia; for he was determined now to make her abandon her enterprise.

"Never lived in a boarding-house before," he thought. "But still I'm sure the atmosphere here isn't the usual thing. Too much ill-will, gossip, so on. Emilia's fault, maybe. Poor girl doesn't know how to cope with people—with anything."

He walked about the house, looking for her, and found her at last in the kitchen; Harly was buttering and slicing bread, and she was supervising this.

"Very thin, Harly."

"Yes, madam."

She smiled at Van Cleef, but she was not, he thought, pleased to see him.

"We'll be having tea in a few moments, Arthur."

"Could we have tea alone?"

She went through the swing-door into the pantry before she answered.

"I can't do things like that, Arthur. It hurts other people's feelings."

"Meaning Bramwell?"

"Well, yes," she admitted. "He's very sensitive."

"Too sensitive. My dear girl, the whole set-up is wrong. Impossible—"

"He's fond of me," she said. "And nobody else is. Nobody else in the world."

Her charming face was incapable of expressing sorrow, even her voice was no more than plaintive.

"I'm fond of you."

"Not very," she said. "You're kind to me, and that's quite different." There was a pile of clean, folded napkins on the shelf; she took them up, one by one, and made another pile of them. "I'm so lonely...." she said, in a low voice. "I'm so lonely...."

"You needn't be, my dear girl. You won't be, if you get away from here. Come to live in town. Different type of life. Friends."

"I have no friends, Arthur."

"That's nonsense, my dear girl. You have any number of friends. I hope I'm one of them."

"There's no one really fond of me but Carlo," she said.

"Even if we admit that, my dear girl, what of it?"

"I can't live without love," she said.

That stopped him for a moment.

"I see," he said presently. "However, you can still come to live in town. Little apartment. Ask your friends to dinner-tea."

"What could I live on?"

"This fellow I told you about will buy the house—"

"I can't give up this house—my—home...."

"But, my dear girl.... This guest-house idea isn't pleasant for you, and it's not profitable."

"It's the only way I can keep my home."

"Home is where the heart is," he said in desperation.

She saw nothing out-of-the way in that.

"My heart is here, Arthur," she said. "Where Bill and I lived—together. I know Bill would want me to live here."

"If you feel like that," he said, "at least you'd better change your guests, my dear girl. Get rid of all of them. We'll find new ones—strangers, this time. Mistake, having friends."

"They're not friends. Not one of them, except Carlo."

"Will you do this?" he asked. "Will you tell the others—all except Carlo, if it has to be that way—that you're going to close the house for a while?"

"Let me think it over, Arthur."

"Don't!" he urged. "Tell them this evening. Get them out, and we'll make a fresh start."

"Please, Arthur, let me think it over."

"Until this evening."

"Yes," she said. "I'll think carefully, Arthur, and I'll tell you this evening."

"Promise?"

"I promise," she said. "Now, here's Harly with the tea. You'll join us—"

"No, thanks!" he said, and then changed his mind. "Better have another look at them," he thought. "Especially Annie."

He was surprised to see Downes in the drawing-room.

"I thought it would do me good," Downes explained. "Lying in bed is weakening."

They all assembled. Mrs. Downes, Miss Carroll, the Major, even Russell; and it was a scene of harmonious politeness.

Russell sat on the floor beside Miss Carroll, and they talked in low tones, paying no attention to anyone else. Annie and Harry Downes sat, one on each side of Van Cleef, talking as they always talked, about little restaurants in Paris, London, Venice, telling bits of news about people he knew or didn't know. The Major sat on the sofa beside Emilia, and was attentive and deferential to her.

"When are you going abroad again, Arthur?" asked Mrs. Downes.

"I don't know," he answered, and he thought, "Never. Why travel just to meet the Downeses somewhere else? I'm better off at home. Home, I said to Emilia, is where the heart is. How true! How do you think of these things, Mr. Van Cleef? Blanche calls me Mr. Van Cleef.... It wouldn't bore her to travel. She'd be happy. She's alive, said please take care of your health... Meaning, can't you lay off the whisky? I wish I had a drink now."

"Mr. Van Cleef!"

It was Major Bramwell standing before him. Van Cleef rose, frowning uneasily beneath the steady glare of those blue eyes.

"Is he going to fly at me?" he thought. "Embarrassing.... Shall I have to knock him down?"

"Mr. Van Cleef! Will you take a drink with me, sir?"

"What's this?" thought Van Cleef.

"I have a small private stock of liquor," the Major went on. "I imported it myself. If you'll do me the honour—"

"Thanks!" said Van Cleef. "Thanks very much!"

"I propose that we go into the conservatory," said the Major.

No one else seemed surprised, or even interested in this invitation; the Major led the way across the drawing-room and opened the glass door into the dusty little wilderness. He closed the door, and even the curtains that covered the glass, Van Cleef noted, were dusty and somehow brittle-looking, like scorched paper.

"I've told the boy to bring both cognac and Scotch," said the Major. "Good quality.... Cigar, sir?"

"Thanks, but I'll stick to cigarettes."

The Major sat down at the bamboo table and cut off the end of a cigar.

"The—er—*amende honorable*," he observed.

"I see," said Van Cleef. Harly came in then, with glasses, two bottles, and a siphon of soda.

"Which do you prefer, sir?" asked the Major.

"Scotch, any day," Van Cleef answered.

"Personally, I prefer cognac. I—er—I'm glad to have this opportunity, sir, to—express my regret for a certain attitude towards you, which was entirely due to a misunderstanding. I apologize."

"Very good of you. Here's wishing you luck!"

They drank.

"What d'you think of the whisky?" asked the Major.

"Oh, excellent!" Van Cleef answered.

The Major began to relate some of his experiences in the Philippines, and Van Cleef sat in unhappy silence; the stories were dusty, stale, melancholy, like the room in which they sat. There was no air....

"Another drink, Van Cleef? Come, come! I insist!"

"No, thanks," said Van Cleef.

He felt sick. Very sick. He sat still while a ghastly nausea came over him like a tide, ebbed, came back; the world swooped up and down, sweat broke out on him, his breath came fast. He was blind now; he could not see the Major, could only hear his voice, very far away.

"Dying...." he thought.

VIII

"Are you feeling better?" she kept on asking. "Are you feeling better now?" She kept on asking it, a hundred, a thousand, a million times, so that, to put an end to it, he came back from somewhere and said, "Yes."

"Drink this, Arthur," she said. "Drink this...." She put her arm under his neck, bending his head forward, and pain shot between his eyes like a knife-thrust.

"Please!" he said.

The rim of a glass touched his teeth. He swallowed what was offered, and she let him lie back again, and have that headache. There was nothing left in the world but that headache, and nausea. He didn't go to sleep; he went spinning round and round in a blackness where little lights whirled.

"Are you feeling better, Arthur?"

He knew now that it was Emilia, miles away.

"Yes," he told her.

"Try to drink this, Arthur...."

It was coffee; the smell of it was sickening.

"Rather—rest, thanks..." he said.

"Just drink this first, Arthur."

He could see her face now, enormous, sorrowful black eyes that grew wider and wider until he was lost in them. Again his head was raised, again with that savage thrust of pain, again he drank to be let alone. But he was getting better. The hot, black coffee was driving out the cold nausea.

"Take one more cup, Arthur...."

She wore a long, pale blue robe, her black hair was loose about her face, she had a cup in one hand, and, he thought, a candle in the other. Coming towards him down an endless corridor, with a candle and a cup of poison.

"Poison...!" he said.

"No. It's coffee, Arthur."

"The dagger, or the bowl..." he said anxiously. He didn't quite understand that; but it was important.

"Please, Arthur, drink it!"

Not a candle; it was a shaded lamp behind her. He drank what she gave him, because he must. Her little fingers clasped his wrist, cold fingers. The wind that blew in at the open window was cold; it was good to breathe.

"Are you better?"

"I'd like a cigarette," he said.

She gave him one, and held a match for him. It made him feel sick and dizzy for a moment, but are you getting better, Arthur, getting better....

"What happened to me?" he asked.

"It's all over now," she said. "Just rest, and you'll feel all right in a little while."

"No," he said, and began remembering. The dusty conservatory, the Major's voice going on and on.... The sun had been shining then, outside the dusty glass, and now it was night....

"What happened, Emilia?"

"It doesn't matter, Arthur, dear...."

"Sorry.... Does matter..." he said. "What happened?"

"Aa-rthur, dear.... Nobody knows, except Carlo and myself, and we'll never mention it."

It was difficult and unpleasant, to think with such a headache.

"Won't mention what?" he asked.

"What happened. It was an accident. We both understand—"

"It wasn't an accident," he said. "Someone gave me something."

"Arthur, don't say that!" she cried. "It's dreadful!"

The thinking was going better now.

"My dear girl," he said, "I've been quite uncomfortable.... I don't like it."

"You didn't realize...."

"Realize what?"

"I've seen Bill like this, often enough," she said.

"You're not trying to say I was drunk, are you?"

"Arthur dear, we both know you didn't realize—"

"I had one drink," he said. "A small one, too."

She said nothing.

"Another cigarette, please," he said. "What time is it? Eleven.... Look here, my dear girl, I had one drink."

"All right, Arthur," she said, with her dainty little smile.

"Does Bramwell say that I had more?"

"I—it doesn't matter in the least, dear."

"I want to see Bramwell. Now."

"He's gone to bed."

"He can get up then."

"Please, Arthur, don't make a scene! It's quite bad enough—"

"I think so. Mind going away for a while? I want to get up."

"Arthur, *please* don't try to see Carlo! He was as kind and nice as possible, getting you up here, without anyone seeing, except Harly.... He understands perfectly."

"Emilia, did he tell you I was drunk?"

"He didn't need to tell me," she said, curtly.

"I'll tell you now that I've been poisoned."

"It hasn't done you much harm," she said, in the same curt tone, a tone he had never before heard her use.

"Still and all, I don't like it," he said. "I don't seem to feel resigned."

"To-morrow morning you'll realize—" she began.

"Sorry, but I'm not going to wait," he said. "Mind leaving me while I get up?"

She turned away, crossed the room; "she took the key out of the lock and, closing the door after her, locked it on the outside.

"*Bien alors!*" he said aloud.

When he got out of bed, it was bad, extremely bad. But anger sustained him. He hadn't felt anger for years; he had forgotten what it was like, what warmth, what energy it gave. He had been undressed, and put into pyjamas by someone; he didn't bother about a dressing-gown; in bare feet, he went into the bathroom and knocked at the door that led to Russell's room.

The boy opened the door promptly.

"What's the matter?" he demanded. "You look like hell."

"Yes. I want to get out through your room."

Russell asked no questions, attempted no interference. Van Cleef went past him and out into the corridor; he knocked at Bramwell's door. He waited; no answer, he knocked again, louder, and the next door opened and Lizzy Carroll came out. For a moment she did not speak, only looked at him, with her thin lips compressed, and pity in her eyes.

"You'd better get back to bed, Arthur," she said in a whisper.

"I have to see Bramwell—"

"Come!" she said, firmly, and took his arm.

He yielded, let her lead him across the corridor, unlock his door, enter with him. He could think of nothing to say that would sound in any way convincing.

"Go to bed, and to sleep, Arthur," she said.

"Lizzy," he said, "I *haven't* been drinking."

"Arthur," she said, with a great compassion, "it's been a good many years since you could say that truthfully."

"I had just one drink this afternoon. This is—something else."

"I have some sleeping-tablets," she said. "They're quite harmless. I'll get you one."

"You don't believe me, Lizzy?"

She regarded him, still with her lips compressed into a thin line.

"No," she said, after a pause. "Get a good night's sleep, Arthur. We can talk things over in the morning. I'll get you a tablet—"

"No, thanks, Lizzy."

"You'd better, Arthur. You don't want to go wandering around the house like this."

"I shan't wander any more, Lizzy."

He lit a cigarette, and she frowned.

"That's dangerous," she said. "Suppose you were to fall asleep?"

"I shan't."

She looked so small and neat, in her flannel dressing-gown, with her red hair in two braids; she looked so anxious and unhappy.... He laid his hand on her shoulder.

"Don't worry, Lizzy," he said. "I shan't wander, or set the house on fire. Or have D.T.s."

She reached up-and kissed his cheek. He was astonished, greatly touched; he put his arm about her shoulders and hugged her.

"Good night, dear!" he said.

"Good night, Arthur!"

He stood staring at the closed door.

"Its-worse than you'd think..." he said to himself. "You get in the habit of being believed. Sort of«shock, not to be."

He went into the bathroom again; the door into Russell's room stood open and he saw the boy, sitting facing him, in his shirt-sleeves, relaxed, sombre.

"What's wrong with you?" Russell asked.

"What d'you think?" asked Van Cleef.

"Take a look in the mirror," said Russell.

"No...."

"When you didn't come down to dinner, I made enquiries," said Russell. "It was all very mysterious. You had indigestion. Mrs. Swan was with you. I came to the door and asked if I could see you. She said you were asleep; but I could hear you muttering. I told her I knew a little about medicine; I pretty well begged her to let me in. But she wouldn't. I waited in here, with the door a little open—and when she went out for a moment, I got in to see you."

Van Cleef went to the window and looked out; the stars were bright and clear in the sky.

"I gave you an antidote," said Russell. "If I hadn't, you'd be dead now."

"Not dead," said Van Cleef. "I think I'll get a spot of sleep, now."

"Do you understand what I've just told you?" cried Russell, springing to his feet. "You were poisoned!"

There was a fierce, blazing look in his dark eyes, an imperious ring in his voice, and it was intolerable; it was like hearing someone shriek.

"'Night!" said Van Cleef.

"Are you going to let the murderer—"

Van Cleef went through the bathroom, into his own room, and locked the door; he sat down on the bed, his hands clasped loosely between his knees.

"No!" he said to himself. "No!"

It was a revulsion almost physical; it was as if he had witnessed a scene of disgusting violence. Then in a little while, he began to think.

"I was going to make it worse.... God! Going to drag out Bramwell, and accuse him.... Yell at him.... Standing out there in pyjamas and bare feet—banging on the door.... I know how I looked to Lizzy."

He got up and went over to the mirror that hung over the chest of drawers; he stood there and looked at himself. His eyes were narrowed, lined at the corners; his face was haggard, pallid; his short, fair hair was wildly ruffled.

"Yes," he said to himself, "that's what I look like—to everyone. That's what I am. Take care of your health, Mr. Van Cleef.... Don't get murdered. You're too valuable." He leaned forward, to look more closely at himself. "Wish you were dead," he said.

His knees felt weak, his head still ached, he still felt sick.

"But it's not much more than a supreme hangover," he thought. "I've felt almost as bad as this, without poison. The murderer is the Major? Bather crude. He's not very bright, but even he... Harly brought in the two bottles. They'd both been opened before; I noticed that. Then we have to assume that the Major planned it all in advance, and that he was reasonably sure I'd take whisky, instead of cognac. Why did he—Well, never mind about motives. He may be jealous. He may be a homicidal maniac. Tried to kill Downes, too. Extremely amateurish work. His victims don't die. But that's because Russell always saves their lives. Russell...."

He sat down and lit a cigarette, and observed that he had one, freshly lighted, lying in an ashtray.

"He knows all about poisons, and antidotes, and everything else..." he thought. "He had the opportunity, along with everyone else in the house. And he's more suitable. Far more suitable. The poisonings begin when he arrives—"

Had they? He remembered what Blanche had told him. Her father called Emilia a murderess.

"What must I do?" he thought. "Suppose I go to the police, and tell them I've been poisoned? Emilia, and Lizzy, probably Harly, and probably Bramwell would swear I was drunk. Then I'd say that, the night before, Downes was poisoned, and he and his wife both deny it. I then go on to say I've heard that Bill Swan was poisoned. At that point, they either kick me out, or lock me up in a padded cell. What must I do?"

For it was clear to him now that he must do something. It was his responsibility. He didn't know why it should be, but he had to acknowledge it.

"I won't be working along with Russell," he thought. "That's very definite. In fact—he's got to go. To-morrow. I think I'm sorry for him; but just the same, he goes. I wonder if there are any of these private detectives? Like in a book.... Quiet, gentlemanly young fellow.... I bring him here as a friend of mine.... Only, where do I find him? And if I did find one of those, and he did get the truth-would I like it? If it's Emilia.... Even if it's Annie Downes, gone queer.... What I want isn't to punish the malefactor. I want to put a stop to this. Downes and I are none the worse. If I can make sure there won't be any more attempts...."

He could think of no possible approach; the whole thing was impossibly difficult, and distressing, and he wanted to be rid of it. He had had no private problems for a long time, a very long time; other people appealed to him, often enough, and he assisted them with money, and with his _ advice, always vague, yet curiously apt. But he hadn't been worried; he bad forgotten how to be worried.

"I want to be let alone..." he thought, irritably. "I can't turn sleuth at this time of life."

He got into bed and turned out the light. Through the window he could see the stars in the sky, very clear and bright. "You'd have been dead," Russell had told him.

"Not very important," he said to himself.

When he closed his eyes, he had a sudden vision of Blanche, standing in the sun. And such regret came to him, such grief, for his youth, his love, for all that was gone....

"I want a drink!" he cried in his heart.

But he did not take one. He lay still, and let that black and bitter tide wash over him, until it was exhausted, and he slept.

The morning was bad. But he had had plenty of bad mornings, and they always passed. He bathed; he shaved with an unsteady hand, he went downstairs, and found no one about except Harly, laying the tables. He watched Harly for a few moments; slim, neat and deft, still a boy. He couldn't actually be a boy; he must be middle-aged, but there was nothing to show that.

"How about Harly?" thought Van Cleef. "He could poison people. And if I keep steadfastly to the homicidal idea, he's as good as anyone. The maniac simplifies things. No bother about motives."

Harly caught sight of him then. "Breakfast, sir?"

"Thanks. Was it you who got me to bed last night, Harly?"

"Yes, sir." Harly was eagerly respectful, as usual; he did not seem at all embarrassed by the question; he stood as if waiting for more.

"That whisky of Major Bramwell's didn't seem to agree with me," Van Cleef went on, tentatively. "Only had one drink, as I remember."

"Yes, sir. Wasn't but one drink gone from the bottle."

"Unusual... I'd like to have a look at that bottle, Harly."

"Major took the bottles up to his own room, sir."

"Where did you get them from yesterday?"

"Major's room, sir."

"Brought them straight to the conservatory?"

"No, sir. Major told me to bring them down before tea; I left them on the sideboard in here, sir, till he'd be ready for them."

"Did you—did the Major ever give you a drink?"

"I'm a teetotaler, sir."

"I don't think it was good whisky."

"No, sir," said Harly.

"Does he mean anything by that?" thought Van Cleef. There was nothing to be read in Harly's face, or in his tone, but he still had an air of waiting alertly. He decided to go on. "Night before last," he said, "I saw a man lurking around the place."

"Yes, sir."

"I thought he might be one of these fellows who sell liquor. They say they've bought it from a ship's steward, something like that, sell it cheap. I wonder if the Major gets his liquor from someone like that?"

"Didn't come to see the Major, sir. Came to see Mr. Downes."

"And did he see Mr. Downes?"

"Yes, sir."

"Did he get into the house?"

"Just into the kitchen, sir. There they had words."

"What words?"

"Didn't say much, sir. Man knocked at the door and gave me an envelope, told me to give it to Mr. Downes. So I took it upstairs—"

"Leave the man alone in the kitchen while you went upstairs?"

"No, sir. Left him outside the back door."

"He could have come in?"

"Yes, sir. I gave the envelope to Mr. Downes, and Mr. Downes, he came downstairs, and he went out to speak to the man. And he came sort of rushing in, and the man after him and pushed Mr. Downes against the wall. Then he saw me in the pantry, and he cursed and went out."

"Mr. Downes say anything?"

"Yes, sir. Mr. Downes said that the man must have been drinking."

"Did you get that impression?"

"No, sir."

"Did you know the man?"

"Yes, sir," said Harly.

"What did you think about the whole thing, Harly?"

"Didn't think, sir," said Harly.

This was somewhat disconcerting.

"Know anything about the man, Harly?"

"Know his name, sir, and where he works."

"You didn't think it was—even interesting, for him to shove Mr. Downes around?"

"Didn't think about it, sir. I have a lot of work to do now, sir, with the cook gone. Too busy to think."

"I suppose you told Mrs. Swan, of course."

"No, sir. I never told anybody but you, sir."

The emphasis on the pronoun puzzled Van Cleef.

"Why me?" he asked.

"Remember you from the old days, sir, when you used to come visiting Mr. Swan. Seemed like you were the right one to tell, sir."

"Ever see the man here before, Harly?"

"Yes, sir. Saw him on the balcony, upstairs."

"What?" said Van Cleef, startled.

"Yes, sir. Was a Sunday afternoon, and most everybody was out. I went around that side of the house—"

"Which side?"

"East, sir. And I saw him climbing down offn the balcony."

"What did you do?"

"Didn't do anything, sir."

"Didn't tell anyone?"

"I told Mrs. Swan, sir, when she came back from the tea-party she was at."

"What did she say?"

"Didn't say anything, sir."

There was a muffled sort of knocking.

"Excuse me, sir, but that's the boy with the eggs," said Harly. "I'll have your breakfast ready in ten minutes, sir."

Van Cleef turned back into the lounge, opened the door, and stepped out on the veranda. It was a sweet morning, fresh and cool.

"It's one thing to get information," he thought, "and it's another thing to have any idea what it means. Dulac the murderer? I'd prefer him not to be, for strictly personal reasons. Blanche wouldn't like it. Seven-thirty.... I suppose she's up now. Maybe this is one of the days when shell want to be a human being, and not go to work...."

He lit a cigarette, and sighed.

"Next step is to inspect the premises," he thought. "Never occurred to me that you could climb down from that balcony. Climb up, too? That would make it more complicated.... I can't suspect Russell wholeheartedly any more. He couldn't very well have had anything to do with Dulac or the balcony, and Dulac shoving Downes around. And Swan...."

There was dew on the grass, and the sun made it glitter. He had seen hundreds of summer mornings, but never, he thought, one so lovely. He turned the corner of the house; a gravel path ran along the side of the veranda and on the opposite side of the path was a rock garden planted by Bill. Like all the things he had left behind, it had turned to dust; there was nothing planted there, only weeds, and the struggling survivors of hardy plants.

And there was something else there this morning. There was a small brown figure, lying on the rocks, flat as a leaf. He ran to it and turned it over.

"Lizzy!" he cried.

She was never going to answer anyone again.

IX

Her face was not disfigured; there was only one small cut on her cheek that had bled a little. She looked composed and quiet, almost amused, her eyes closed, her brown flannel dressing-gown belted neatly about her waist. Her hand was cold, but not stiff.

"Lizzy..." he said. "My dear girl...."

She looked so *little*.... He rose from his knees beside her, and stood looking down at her for a time. The sun shone in her face, he covered it with his handkerchief. Then he went to the back door, and entered the kitchen. Harly was at the stove.

"Harly," he said, "Telephone for whatever doctor comes here. And send for the police. There's been an accident to Miss Carroll."

Harly stared at him with his mouth open, suddenly become stupid, idiotic.

"Telephone—" Van Cleef began.

"Yes, sir!" said Harly, becoming alert again.

Van Cleef went back to Lizzy Carroll.

"How long has she been alone?" he thought. "I was talking to Harly—I was so near.... When did this happen to her?"

Then he thought with a shock, "*How* did this happen to her?"

He looked up at the balcony, and he saw that part of the iron railing had carried away; all of it was eaten with rust.

"Leaned against it and fell?" he asked himself.

It didn't matter much, now. She was gone, and in his heart was the feeling that she had gone too soon, before she was ready.

"Enjoyed life," he thought. "Knew how to live. I wish she could have known I wasn't drunk last night.... But she was still my friend...."

The breeze stirred the hem of her nightdress beneath the dressing-gown; her feet were bare; narrow little feet.

"Oh, God! I'm sorry!" he said to her.

He took out a cigarette, but he did not light it.

"She wouldn't like me to smoke," he thought. "She'd say: 'I did think you'd have enough self-control not to smoke beside my dead body.'"

Harly came out to him; stopped with a very hasty glance at Miss Carroll.

"Dr. Robinson is coming, sir, and the police. Shall I tell Mrs. Swan?"

"I wouldn't know..." said Van Cleef, frowning. He felt that perhaps he should be the one to tell Emilia, but he was not going to leave Lizzy Carroll lying out here alone. "She'd hate it," he thought. Harly was waiting. "Better tell her, Harly," he said, and Harly went.

Van Cleef stood in the path, a lonely sentinel, hands in his pockets, his head bent, his big shoulders hunched, so lost in his meditations upon this friend that he did not hear a car come up the drive, did not notice the appearance of a man until a voice spoke:

"I'm Doctor Robinson."

A jaunty fellow, Doctor Robinson was, neat and slim, with a little toothbrush moustache, and a bow tie; youngish, with bright brown eyes.

"Name's Van Cleef. An old friend of Miss Carroll's."

The doctor knelt beside Miss Carroll, and Van Cleef strolled off a little way down the path. He waited until he heard the doctor's step behind him.

"D'you know how this happened, Mr. Van Cleef?" he asked, with a pleasant smile.

"No," said Van Cleef, resenting that smile.

A door banged, someone came running down the steps of the veranda. Emilia came running round the corner of the house. She wore a green linen blouse with long sleeves, a pleated black skirt; she ran daintily in her high-heeled pumps.

"Doctor *Robinson*!" she cried, and caught his sleeve. "It's suicide!"

"Emilia!" said Van Cleef, aghast.

"It's suicide!" she repeated, looking fervently into the doctor's face. And he continued smiling pleasantly. They were incredible.

"Of course, if you have any information, Mrs. Swan, the police—"

"Do the police have to come?"

"I'm afraid so."

"I—saw her do it...."

"Emilia," said Van Cleef, again, "come into the house."

"I want to tell Doctor Robinson first—"

"No."

"I must, Arthur! It's important! I saw poor Lizzy—"

The doctor looked at Van Cleef, still with that unfading smile, but his bright eyes were serious.

"I think it would be advisable to go into the house, Mrs. Swan," he said. "The police will be—occupied here...." Still smiling, he took her hand from his sleeve, and laid it upon Van Cleef's arm, as if making him a present. "And, y'see, your evidence will be of vital importance, Mrs. Swan. Miss Carroll was not killed by the fall."

"Not..."

"No, oh, no!" he said.

"Then what?"

"There'll be an enquiry," he said, "And—" he paused, "I'd be inclined to say that Miss Carroll has been lying here for some time," he said. "An hour—possibly longer." He obviously intended that she should get that clear in her mind. "At least an hour," he said.

"Come on, Emilia!" said Van Cleef.

She walked by his side to the front of the house.

"Where, Arthur?" she asked.

"Conservatory," he answered, and they went in there; he closed the door. "Emilia, don't tell that story to the police."

"What story, Arthur?"

"Don't say you saw Lizzy commit suicide."

"I—I thought I did," she said, faintly.

"Where were you when 'you thought you did'? Where could you be, to see the balcony outside her room?"

"Arthur!" she cried. "Please.... I—only thought it would be better—"

"For whom?"

"For—everyone. It's so horrible—when the police come.... Everything—the most private things—all dragged out...." She stood with her hand on the back of a chair, her lashes lowered. "I'm sure, Lizzy herself wouldn't like—all that publicity...."

"Nothing to worry about in Lizzy's private life," Van Cleef said, briefly. And all the time he was thinking: "She never looked at Lizzy. Never even turned her head. Not once."

"Arthur, she was older than she admitted. She was forty-two. I know that."

He looked away from her.

"Arthur.... Please!"

"I'm sorry," he said. "I can't understand you."

"Oh, please don't say that!" she cried, with such anguish that he was startled.

"I don't. I can't," he said.

"I thought you did. I never know how to explain things. I never have."

"Explain?"

"I'm—fighting for my life!" she said.

"Emilia!"

"I am! I am!"

"But how? What do you-" The doorbell rang. "Don't tell that story to the police!" he said, in haste. "For God's sake, don't tell them any lies. You'll make it worse for yourself."

"I couldn't. I wish I was dead."

"Sergeant Warren is here, madam."

"Show him in," said Van Cleef, before she could speak.

Sergeant Warren entered, a stout man, bald, with an ivory-coloured face of severe calm.

"Mrs. Swan?" he said. "Like to ask you a few questions, madam." He glanced at Van Cleef.

"I'm the one who found the—found Miss Carroll."

"That so?" said the Sergeant, raising his almost invisible eyebrows. "Then maybe you'll give me a little information.... Name—occupation—no occupation?—age—address.... Did you note the posture of the body, Mr. Van Cleef? Did you move, or in any way disturb—Were you acquainted with the deceased?"

"Yes, I've known her for years."

"When did you last see deceased?"

"Last night—about eleven."

"What was the occasion?"

"I wasn't felling well, and Miss Carroll asked if she could do anything for me."

"What impression did you get about Miss Carroll? Was she cheerful, for instance?"

"Yes," he answered, curtly, "Miss Carroll was just as usual."

"She wasn't in unusually high spirits, for instance?"

"She was not."

"You state you've known deceased for years. Did you ever have reason to think she was addicted to the use of any drug, or drugs?"—

"I'd take an oath that she was not."

"How is that? Did you ever discuss the subject with her? Ever hear her mention any drug, or drugs?"

Then Van Cleef remembered that she had offered him a sleeping-tablet; quite harmless, she had said. The Sergeant was waiting for an answer, but he took his time.

"No!" he said, at last. "Nobody who knew Miss Carroll would think for a moment that she was addicted to drugs; she was a woman of courage and—highest character."

The Sergeant wrote something in a notebook; Van Cleef wondered if he were writing that Lizzy had been a woman of courage, and the highest character. He glanced up.

"This may be important," he explained. "It may be that you were the last to see deceased alive." He asked a few more questions, then he turned to Emilia. Her name? Her age? Thirty-seven. Occupation?

"I take paying guests," she answered, and Van Cleef wondered if the Sergeant wrote that down verbatim.

Had she known deceased long? Yes, for years. Ten years at least. When had she last seen deceased? A little after dinner, last night. Had Miss Carroll seemed to her in good spirits?

"No," said Emilia, "she was very much depressed. She said she had a bad headache. I asked her if she wanted some aspirin, and she said she had something better than that."

"Say what it was she had?"

"No. She was always very nervous, and highly-strung."

"Would you say she was subject to fits of depression?"

"Yes."

"Did she, to your knowledge, have any financial, or other worries?"

"I know she was worried about *something*."

Van Cleef turned his back, lit a cigarette, and looked out through the dusty panes.

"Fighting for her life?" he thought. "And this is the way she's 'fighting.'... Against a dead woman." At the first moment of silence, he turned to the Sergeant. "There'll be an autopsy, won't there?"

"Yes. Now, Mrs. Swan, can you give the name or names of deceased's nearest relatives?"

"She didn't have anyone, much," Emilia answered. "She always said she liked the friends she picked out better than the relatives that had been picked out for her. I can give you the names—"

"I was an old friend," said Van Cleef. "I'll look after the arrangements. I'll get in touch with her lawyer, Ross. Know him well. Finished with me?"

"For the moment. There'll be an inquest. We'll notify you."

"Au revoir!" said Van Cleef, and went off across the drawing-room, to the hall. He saw Annie Downes in the dining-room, alone.

"Arthur!" she said, raising her voice. He went to her table, and she patted the chair next to her. "Sit down with me?" she said. "Harry went back to bed when he heard.... Any sort of shock gives him this dreadful nervous indigestion."

"Not—bad, is he?" asked Van Cleef.

"Oh, no! Harly's taking him a tray. If he rests, he's always better. Isn't it a sad thing? Poor Lizzy!"

"Very dangerous, that balcony," said Van Cleef, glancing sidelong at her. "Railing's crumbling away."

"Do you think the fall killed her?" asked Mrs. Downes.

"What else?"

"I thought that perhaps she had one of her heart attacks.... She suffered so horribly with them. Angina, you know."

"I didn't know."

"I was with her once, when she had one. I remember there was some sort of capsule she told me to-break and hold under her nose. I was very thankful that Harry wasn't there. He can't stand the sight of suffering."

Harly brought their breakfast; Van Cleef drank black coffee.

"There'll be an autopsy," he thought. "The police will find out the truth. Not my job, thank God!"

He had no theory as to how Lizzy Carroll had died; he made no attempt to form one, he did not want to form one. The thing that mattered was, that she shouldn't be slandered.

"Too early to catch Ross," he thought, looking at his watch. He went upstairs with Mrs. Downes; she went to see her ailing Harry, and Van Cleef went into his own room. The bed was not yet made; the place had somehow a debauched look in the morning sun; two unemptied ash-trays, two bottles of whisky on the chest of drawers.

"I need a drink," he thought. He took up the open bottle and stared at it, and set it down; with a sigh that lifted the leaden oppression from his heart, he thought of Blanche. It seemed to him that everyone else was old, sad, timid; and only she was young and honest, and brave. It was a good world, if she were alive in it. "Suppose Mr. Van Cleef did 'take care of his health'?" he asked himself. "He was a sick man last night, but here he is alive. What are you going to do about being alive, Mr. Van Cleef?" There was a knock at the door. "Come in!" he said, and in came Russell. He had forgotten Russell, and it was no pleasure to be reminded of him.

"Better go home," he suggested. "Mean to say there's plenty of trouble here for Mrs. Swan. The fewer people in the house, the better."

Russell sat down on the unmade bed.

"There's more trouble on the way," he said.

"You think,"

"I know," said Russell.

He looked sulky and miserable; and Van Cleef felt sorry for him.

"Look here!" he said, with a somewhat anxious smile. "I've been a bit short-tempered with you. Sorry. You've tried to be helpful. Only—I wish you wouldn't be. I—Miss Carroll was a friend of mine. It's upsetting.... The rest of it doesn't interest me at the moment."

"It certainly doesn't interest me," said Russell. "It's turned out to be so damned obvious. But I was afraid you'd be unhappy if any more of your friends got murdered."

"There haven't been any murders. Hold on! Let me finish! I'll admit that someone gave me something unpleasant, and apparently to Downes, too. Whether with intent to kill or not, I don't know, and neither do you. I'm not making light of the situation. It's ugly. I'm going to put it to an end in the only possible way, and that is, by breaking up the group here."

"That will be too late. There's a killer loose here," said Russell.

"Meaning a fiend who's going to go on poisoning people? No. Sorry. That doesn't click. I feel I'd recognize a fiend if I met him."

"You've met the killer."

"Potential killer, maybe. As I pointed out, nobody knows whether or not Downes and myself were meant to die."

"Miss Carroll's dead."

"She's dead. And the police will look after that."

"I've just been talking to Doctor Robinson. He knows my uncle, and for that reason he was indulgent to my boyish curiosity. There's going to be an autopsy. But no analyses."

"No analyses.... Oh, I see what you mean."

"They'll find exactly what Robinson intends to find; a diseased condition of the heart. He treated Miss Carroll for that. He was almost ready to give a certificate without a post-mortem, when Mrs. Swan began talking about suicide."

"I see what you're getting at, of course. Forget it."

"She was murdered," said Russell.

"*Will* have someone murdered, won't you? No.... Forget it. Go back to town now.... I'll see you there in a few days, when this is over."

"My God!" cried Russell. "Isn't there *anything* I can do? I know that woman was murdered, and I know how she was murdered. I tried to tell that grinning fool of a doctor. I'm trying to tell you. But nobody—"

Van Cleef rose, and laid his hand on the boy's shoulder.

"Take it easy!" he said, with a sort of gentleness. "Mistake to think everyone else is a fool. Dangerous mistake. Go home, and leave this to the doctor and the police."

The boy sat motionless, a blank look on his face. Van Cleef withdrew his hand and lit a cigarette.

"Oh, get out!" he cried in his heart.

The boy rose.

"I've tried to tell you," he said. "I've tried to warn you. There's been one murder done, and there's going to be another." He paused. "Unless you'll listen to me," he said.

"Look here!" said Van Cleef. "You're getting a bit pathological. Mean to say, it's bad, it's dangerous, to be the one person on earth who's always right. I'll have a word with Doctor Robinson, and if there's anything amiss in Miss Carroll's death, he'll find it out. Not your headache. Hop into your car, and drive home."

"Home?" said Russell with a smile. "All right! I'll go. You can enjoy the next murder in peace."

X

Harly came in to make the bed and Van Cleef stood aside, watching him. Harly didn't look at him, and did not talk, would not suddenly begin to talk.

"Too much talking," thought Van Cleef. "I'm going to stay shut up here until it's time to ring up Ross. Then I'll have a word with Robinson. Then I'll have a drink." He moved aside for the carpet-sweeper Harly was pushing. "Suppose I never took another drink? Would I go to pieces, or would I turn into something else? What else? Nothing probably. Probably too late."

Harly dropped the carpet-sweeper against the wall, and hastened out of the room; a telephone bell was ringing.

"Lot more talking to be done," thought Van Cleef. "I'll have to talk Emilia into closing this house. I don't feel like talking to her, ever again. Or seeing her."

"Telephone for you, sir," said Harly.

"Where's the telephone?"

"In the lounge, sir."

The Major was sitting in the lounge, reading a newspaper; he looked over it with his usual glare.

"Good morning, sir!" he said, challengingly. "I hear that imputations have been made—"

"Sorry!" said Van Cleef, and took up the receiver. "Hello!"

"Mr. Van Cleef?"

"None other," he said.

Strange, to hear *her* voice.

"Could I possibly see you?"

"Anything wrong, Blanche?" he said, alarmed.

"Yes," she said.

"I'll come," he said, and hung up the receiver.

"Arthur," said Mrs. Downes, "I must speak to you."

She was standing beside him with her knitting in her hand, a faintly annoyed look on her mild face.

"Got to run along to the village just now," he said, apologetically. "But I'll be back—"

"I must speak to you *before* you see Blanche," said she, in a low voice. "It's important."

"All right!" he said. "I'll be back in a moment."

"I'll meet you in the conservatory," said she.

He ran upstairs to Russell's room, found the boy there reading a pamphlet.

"Care to drive me down to the village in ten minutes?" he asked.

"Yes," Russell answered sullenly, and Van Cleef ran down the stairs again, and went to the conservatory, that spot, he thought, destined for unwelcome confidences.

"Annie's a dark horse," he thought. "Or is it a dark sheep?"

He had absolutely no curiosity as to what she might say, no interest. And he was not worried about Blanche, not disturbed; only impatient and strangely elated.

"Thought of me when something went wrong," he said to himself.

Annie Downes was sitting in a wicker chair, her eyes upon her swift-moving knitting needles.

"I happened to hear you say 'Blanche,'" she said. "I wondered if you knew?"

"Knew what?"

"I only found out, a little while ago," she went on. "But it seems that poor Lizzy knew, and I imagine the Major knows."

"Don't get you, Annie."

"About Blanche," she said. "Do you know who she is, Arthur?"

"No...."

"She's Bill Swan's child," said Mrs. Downes.

"Is that a rumour?"

"No, it's a fact. When I found out, I talked it over with poor Lizzy. She'd known from the beginning, but she and I didn't see it in the same light."

"How did Lizzy know?"

"She was here when the mother—Mrs. Dulac died. There was a frightful scene, she said. Dulac came, threatening to shoot Bill, and so on. He said his wife had been murdered."

"Like everybody else..." said Van Cleef.

"What's that, Arthur?"

"Sorry! Nothing.... How did you find out about this, Annie?"

"I can't tell you that, Arthur. But as soon as I did find out, I looked up the child. I asked her here, I talked to her. It's an outrage!"

"What is?"

Her eyes looked cold behind her glasses.

"She's a charming child—Bill's own daughter—and simply abandoned in poverty, and misery—"

"Hardly—"

"That Dulac is a *workman* of some sort! The child's had no education, no advantages. She doesn't even know the truth about herself."

"Better off, not knowing."

"Arthur, how can you say that? Is it better for her to think she's the daughter of a common workman, instead of Bill Swan's daughter?"

"Very much better."

"You're like Lizzy," she said. "That's what Lizzy said. But I don't agree. In Norway, or is it Sweden...?"

"Couldn't say."

"Well, in some country like that, they have a law.... There's no such thing as an illegitimate child. That's only just. It's not a child's fault."

"Did you tell Blanche?" he asked.

"No, I haven't. I *wanted* to tell her, and I think she has a *right* to know; but to be frank, Arthur, I didn't dare to tell her. I was afraid for my life."

"Annie!" he protested.

"Arthur," she said, leaning forward, "you don't *know* that woman! There's nothing she'd stop at, to gain her ends. Nothing! She wouldn't let Bill do anything for his child—"

"How do you know?"

"I do know. She wouldn't let Bill do anything. And she deliberately disregarded Bill's dying wishes."

"Annie, how do you know all this?"

"I can't tell you. But it's *all* true. With his dying breath, Bill asked Emilia to look after Blanche. And she promised that she *would*. She's—infamous!"

"No!"

"Arthur Van Cleef," she said, "you're a fool!"

She folded her arms and looked at him, exactly like a severe school teacher.

"You're a fool!" she repeated. "You, and Major Bramwell, both of you...."

He was silent for a moment.

"Annie.... I've been thinking quite a bit, lately.... Whole set-up is bad.... Why don't you and Downes clear out, at once?"

She began to cry. She rose, letting her knitting fall to the floor; she stepped on it as she opened the door.

"I wish," she said, "I wish the house—would burn down— with her in it!"

The door closed after her.

"So that's it?" he said to himself.

It seemed to him obvious that what so troubled Annie Downes was not his folly, and not Bramwell's.

"Must be Harry," he thought. "Is Emilia a Circe? Can't see it...."

He sat down, wanting and needing a few moments to think.

"It could be true about Blanche," he thought. "I wish it wasn't. I wish, anyhow, that she'd never have to know. Papa Dulac hasn't done badly by her. Better maybe than Bill ever would have done.... Bather fine thing for Papa Dulac to do. Bring up another man's child. Bring her up to be the honest, darling kid she is...."

"It's fifteen minutes," said Russell, opening the door. "I thought you'd want to be reminded."

"Yes, thanks. *Allons!*"

"Where?"

"Leave me at the railway station, will you? I have some telegrams to send."

Russell smiled.

"All right! I'll wait for you—in the stationer's," he said, and said it with malice.

"On second thoughts," said Van Cleef, evenly, "I'll stop at the stationer's first. I want to speak to Blanche."

"She has a nice French sense of finance," Russell observed.

"Meaning—?"

"I called on her yesterday. And she asked me how much money you had; and if you were in love with anyone."

Van Cleef waited before he spoke.

"Well..." he said. "You're going home to-day; and after this, I won't have to believe in your existence."

"You're right. You can kick me back into limbo. You can hate me. I'm used to it. And, by God! this is the last time I'll ever try to—" He stopped, with a gasp like a sob. "Ever try to make a friend. I can't do it. I've tried—with you—"

"Why do you always spoil everything—?" Van Cleef began, half-angry, and wholly distressed.

"Because that's the way I'm made," said Russell, fiercely. "I have to 'spoil everything.' When I found you again, I thought I'd be different. But I thought you'd be different, too. I thought you'd be the one human creature I could be honest with, and I was honest. I gave myself away, completely. I told you my faults. And you hate me for them, like everyone else."

"I don't hate you!" cried Van Cleef, exasperated. "You're a pest, that's all. You say things you know damn well I won't like, and when I don't like them, you call it 'hate.' You— you goad me. That's the word for it."

"A pest..." said Russell. "I'm not a fool, though. I've found out, without any help from anyone, what's happened in that house. I did it on your account, because the people are friends of yours. You won't believe me, and you won't listen to me. You've simply kicked me out."

It was bad, altogether bad, thought Van Cleef, to feel as he did towards the boy. If it wasn't hate, it was something very like it.

"About that," he said. "It's in the hands of the police, now. They'll find out whatever's essential."

"I don't think so," said Russell. "There's one essential fact that's been obvious all the time, yet no one's noticed it. Miss Carroll was an intelligent woman, and she didn't notice it. You haven't noticed it. I don't think the police will notice it. A beautiful case of persecution mania."

"What?" asked Van Cleef, sharply.

"Someone with well-developed delusions of persecution. Anyone who knows even the rudiments of psychology, knows the dangers of those delusions."

"You mean... Who's got these delusions?"

"Bramwell," said Russell.

Van Cleef considered this, with interest, and a vast relief.

"Persecution?" he said, presently.

"You've heard him, and seen him. What grievance he had against Downes. I don't know—although I can guess it. But your offence is plain enough."

"Yes," said Van Cleef; but Russell was not to be stopped. "He's jealous of you, of course. I imagine he was jealous of Downes. As for Miss Carroll it was her radio—"

"No. That won't do. Too trivial."

"He's not sane," said Russell. "He was convinced that she was deliberately annoying him. She wasn't any too gentle with him, either."

"You think he killed her?"

"I do. His room is next to hers. All he had to do was step out on the balcony, to reach her room."

"Walks in through the window, and offers her a dose of poison."

"It's not difficult to think of something more reasonable than that. How about her being asleep, with a glass or a jug of water beside her?"

"Don't care much for that. She has her own bathroom. Most people will get fresh water, instead of taking what has been standing beside them."

"You'll admit it's possible, though."

"All right. For the sake of argument, Bramwell puts poison in a glass of water, and she drinks it. Dies immediately."

"No. From what I was able to observe, I'd say she's been given an overdose of some barbital preparation. She probably died in her sleep."

"I hope so..." said Van Cleef, half to himself. "I hope so...." He frowned, and glanced up. "What's your idea about the fall from the balcony?"

"He wasn't sure she was dead. And he intended to make sure."

"Threw her off?"

"That seems obvious."

"No...." Van Cleef said. "I don't seem to care for the details.... But this persecution mania thing might be looked into."

"I agree with you," said Russell, with a half-smile. "Just as well to look into it—before there's another killing."

"You'd better take your theory to the police."

"No."

"If you think the fellow's dangerous—"

"It's my duty," said Russell. "My duty to go to the police, and be sneered at. When my 'theory' is proved to be fact, I'll get no credit. I'm a half-baked young fool, with too much money and not enough work."

"I'll tell the police, then."

"Tell them what? There's no evidence, yet. They'll be civil to you, and that's all. There's only one thing you can do. You can tell Doctor Robinson you want analyses made, to determine the presence of poison. He'll do it for you."

"I'll think it over."

"Better not think too long."

"Next chapter entitled: 'The Killer Strikes Again.' Maybe.... I'll think it over."

"You don't accept my theory?"

"Don't know. I've got to think. But I'll keep an eye on the Major. Don't worry. I'll see that you get credit—if you're right. You can tool back to the city with an easy mind."

"Do you object very much, if I stay one more night?"

"I do! I do!" thought Van Cleef. "Mustn't be arbitrary, though. Who do you think is the next candidate for the Major's attention?" he asked, aloud.

"I couldn't say. He's in a condition in which any sort of fancied grievance will do."

"May not find any grievance for days, weeks...."

"He'll find one immediately. You've got to remember that the man's a homicidal maniac. He's killed once, and got away with it. He'll try again, probably to-night."

"Well keep an eye on him," said Van Cleef.

"You're not taking it too seriously, are you?"

"I told you I wanted to think it over," said Van Cleef, with a kind of sternness. "There's something—"

"What 'something'?"

Something in the background of Van Cleef's mind that eluded him. Something he couldn't remember, or perhaps couldn't understand, just yet. He wanted to be left in peace for a while.... But they were in the village, now, and the thought of Blanche came, and blotted out everything else.

"She wouldn't ask me to come, unless it were important. She's a self-reliant kid.... Has she found out—what Annie told me? No, she wouldn't send for me for that. She'd—I don't know how she'd take that. But I think it would hurt. No matter how sensible, and modern, and what not she is; that would hurt.... I don't like her to be hurt...."

"Want me to wait?" asked. Russell.

"D'you mind?"

"I haven't anything to do," said Russell. He parked the car beside the railway station, settled down comfortably behind the wheel, and Van Cleef crossed the street to the dim little shop.

She was standing before, the shelves of that very modest "Lending Library," rearranging the books; in a sleeveless dress of dark green linen she looked tall and slight, cool as a dryad. At the sound of his step, she turned her head.

"Oh!" she said, unsmiling, "Do you want to take a book out, Mr. Van Cleef?"

"Thanks, yes," he said, approaching the shelves.

"This is a good one," she said, and pressed something into his hand. "You'll like to read this, after you get home. That'll be a dollar deposit, and twenty-five cents for each book, which you may keep out for one week."

He put his hand into his pocket to take out his bill-fold, and to put in the paper she had given him. Maybe there was someone watching. Or maybe she was making a mystery out of nothing. Whatever it was, he was more than willing to play up to her.

"I understand the terms," he said. "Thanks for recommending a book."

He smiled, but not she; her grey eyes were troubled, he thought she was pale; he thought, with alarm, that she was very unhappy.

"I'm a quick reader," he said. "I'll probably bring the book back to-morrow."

"There's more to it than you think," she said. Someone else came in to buy cigarettes. "Good-bye!" she said to Van Cleef, and he went out into the street.

"I'll send my telegram," he said to Russell. "Shan't be long."

There was nobody in the waiting-room, even the ticket office was closed. He took out the paper she had handed to him, opened it, and an enclosure fell out. He snatched it up in haste.

Dear Mr. Van Cleef: was written on nice blue paper, in a clear, small hand, I got the enclosed note, this morning. Please take it seriously. There isn't time to think over this. I can only write what comes into my head. I am afraid you don't care what happens to you, but I care, terribly. If that makes any difference, please look after yourself. God bless you.

Your friend,
Blanche.

He had not known that he could feel so keen a pain. His heart had been numb so long.... He put her letter into his pocket, and looked at the enclosure. It was made of letters and words cut from a newspaper, and pasted to make a message. "Do not trust V.C. If he continues seeing you he will be killed."

He put that into his pocket, too, and went into the telegraph office. This was for Russell's benefit only; he sent an entirely superfluous telegram to his hotel. "Returning in a few days will notify." Then he went into a telephone booth to call up Ross, his lawyer and Miss Carroll's; in his halting fashion, he gave an account of what had happened.

"Cause of death isn't determined yet," he said. "Better come out, don't you think?"

Hanging up the receiver, he thought for a while. "Police?" he asked himself, and presently answered himself. "Not yet."

XI

"Any other errands?" asked Russell.

"None."

"Want to stop somewhere for a drink?"

"No drink just now."

No drink would serve him now, he thought. He could not get back into the shadow of vagueness; he had been stabbed into life, and he had to endure it.

"You'll see the doctor, won't you?"

"The doctor?" he replied, frowning. "Why? Nothing wrong—"

"About getting the analyses made," said Russell, impatiently; and Van Cleef answered him with equal impatience:

"I said I wanted to think it over. Give me a little peace, can't you?"

Russell turned sulky then, and began to drive faster and faster. The indicator showed seventy-five.

"Slow down!" said Van Cleef.

Russell laughed and went on, swerving round a corner, and there was a furniture van before them, looking like a house. Van Cleef had a glimpse of the driver's face, stupid with fear; the car swerved sideways across the road, splintered through a fence into a garden. The van driver stopped to yell curses at the boy; backing the car out on the road, Russell called back an insult of startling obscenity, and was off again.

"Sorry I frightened you," he said, glancing at Van Cleef, his dark face alive and joyous.

"Have you ever been caught?" asked Van Cleef, slowly.

"No. Only chased. That's magnificent!"

"Never had to pay, yet, for anything, have you?"

"Never."

"Some day you'll get a bill," said Van Cleef; and Russell laughed again.

They were silent for a time.

"If I'd been killed," Van Cleef thought, "she'd have been sorry.... Who sent her that note? Was it Bramwell? How could it be Bramwell? How would he know that I was interested in Blanche? Easy. Someone could have told him. But why should he object? If he's jealous of me on Emilia's account, he'd be pleased.... Doesn't make sense, for him to have sent it. But suppose he's so crazy that nothing he does makes sense? No.... If he was as bad as that, I'd have noticed it. Emilia would have noticed it. Everyone would have noticed it. If a lawyer, or a doctor asked me questions—Did you notice anything remarkably peculiar in Bramwell's behaviour? Sure he's peculiar, but not more than most people. I've met much queerer birds. He impressed me as a pompous, cantankerous old ass, of which there are plenty. Maniac? Homicidal maniac? There's only Russell's word for that."

He glanced at Russell, and found his face serene and happy.

"Thing is, that Russell's theory is the only one that fits. There can't be any other one person in the house who'd have it in for Downes and myself and Lizzy. How about three separate murderers? Or how about no murderers, and no murder? That's the crux of the whole thing. If Lizzy was poisoned, then there's a case. I'll have to see Doctor Robinson. I'll ring him up later, when I'm alone." He frowned, surprised at himself. "There you are!" he thought. "It's the boy's own idea, but I don't want to admit I'm even considering it. This must be what we call human nature.... Petty. Very low." He sighed. "We might stop and see Doctor Robinson," he observed.

"Do we know where he lives?"

"We make enquiries."

They asked a postman, and got directions; they drove to the doctor's house, but he was out; his wife wrote down a message, asking him to ring up Van Cleef.

"I'll tell Boss," Van Cleef thought. "Trained legal mind.... Never believes anything.... His business, to give advice. How does he feel, when it turns out to be wrong? A bit sheepish?"

They turned into the drive, and the sight of the house brought his drifting thoughts into focus.

"Where's Lizzy?" he thought. "Poor little thing...."

Harly opened the door for them, and as they entered, Van Cleef thought that the very air had changed; this house in which no one was young had always been quiet, but now it was hushed. Russell ran up the stairs, and Van Cleef, at a loss, wandered into the drawing-room. Nobody there. Where were they all? What were they doing?

"Van Cleef!" said Bramwell's voice. "I'd like a few words with you."

He had put on a black tie; his blue eyes still glared in his ruddy face, but he had a subdued voice.

"Oh, yes...!" Van Cleef said.

"Perhaps you'll take a drink with me?"

"Thanks, no..." Van Cleef answered, surprised. This was, surely, the most naive poisoner ever known.

"I propose that we walk in the grounds," said the Major. "I have a certain communication to make...."

This, thought Van Cleef, was a unique opportunity to study the Major; the only drawback was his own sense of inadequacy for making such a study. They went out of the house and on to the lawn, where they began to pace, side by side, Van Cleef tall, loose-jointed, hands in his pockets, the Major straight and stiff.

"In this crisis," said the Major, "I feel—very much alone, Van Cleef."

Van Cleef glanced sidelong at him, still more surprised.

"We are, comparatively speaking, strangers," the Major went on. "But there's the—er—freemasonry that exists among men of the world...." He paused a moment. "You, as a man of the world, will be able to understand my—er— point of view.... A cigar?" He lit one for himself. "I've had a talk with Emilia," he said. "I was able to persuade her to withdraw her unfortunate—her most unfortunate remarks to

Robinson and the Sergeant. I must say they both understood the—er—conditions that prompted her. Hysterical...."

"I don't quite follow...."

"Emilia retracted what she had said relative to Miss Carroll's death being suicidal. I—reasoned with her. I endeavoured to point out the—the injustice of this. Injustice to a woman for whom, in spite of certain differences of opinion, I had, and have, a profound respect," said the Major. "I am absolutely certain that Miss Carroll would never, in any circumstances, have taken her own life."

"Then you think the thing was—"

"An accident. Absolutely. Doctor Robinson fully agrees. Our reconstruction of the tragedy is this. Miss Carroll suffered one of her heart attacks and either went out upon the balcony or was already there when attacked. The attack proved fatal; she fell against the railing, which gave way."

"Doctor agrees with that?"

"Entirely! There is no alternative explanation. It was certainly not suicide, and it was certainly not murder."

"Why 'certainly'?"

"Who'd murder Miss Carroll?" asked the Major. "And how? Her door was locked on the inside. Nobody could have entered her room by the window except myself or Emilia, and you will agree that no sane person would suspect either of us. No. It's unquestionably an accident."

"Is this the cunning of a madman?" thought Van Cleef.

"Emilia's conduct is easy to understand," said the Major, "and—for us, at least—easy to condone. She's never recovered from the ordeal of—er—Swan's death, and she was panic-stricken at the thought of a recurrence of those monstrous suspicions. A highly-strung, intensely sensitive nature.... Not—er—logical."

"I'm not so sure about that," thought Van Cleef. "Has her own kind of logic, maybe."

"The problem now," said the Major, "is to prevent Downes from making his—his outrageous confession."

"Confession?"

"He wants to tell the police!" cried the Major. "Most disgusting cowardice.... He says he'd prefer to go to jail and be done with it. My God, sir! I could cheerfully shoot that—scoundrel!"

They had stopped walking; Van Cleef looked at the other in stupefaction.

"You're amazed," said the Major. "I don't wonder, sir. You're, of course, acquainted with all the circumstances of that deplorable affair, and you know as well as I do that Emilia can't be considered *morally* responsible for what she did. She was overwrought. She's—impulsive. But the fact remains, that she's *legally* responsible, and if that scoundrel does go to the police with his story, she can be charged with criminal conspiracy. It's possible—it's even probable— that she might be sent to prison. He's got to be stopped!"

"Let's go over it, point by point," said Van Cleef. "Let's see exactly what there is against Emilia...."

"But it's, unfortunately, only too plain," said the Major. "She's never attempted to deny that she destroyed Swan's will. You and I understand her temperament, but in a court of law... I've thought and thought over it... It's my belief that the only defence would be to prove she had been temporarily insane."

"Ha!" said Van Cleef, as if he had had a blow in the midriff.

"It's not pleasant," the Major agreed. "But there's a good deal of truth in it. When the poor girl saw that will—when she learned for the first time about that illegitimate daughter of Swan's, it undoubtedly threw her off balance. You can picture it.... There's her husband lying dead. Terrific shock to her. She comes across the will in his desk, acknowledging this girl, bequeathing her a share in his estate.... It's nothing short of a calamity that she turned to that scoundrel Downes at that moment."

"Might be established that she'd acted under his influence," said Van Cleef, carefully.

"Not while Annie Downes is able to speak," said the Major. "She, of course, is going to assert exactly the opposite opinion. Going to declare that Downes was led astray by Emilia. It's been—ghastly—to watch that woman ferreting out the truth. I don't know what put her on the track. Probably Downes himself, with some unpardonable stupidity. Anyhow, she's got the whole story now, and, upon my word, I believe she'd gladly see her husband go to prison if Emilia could suffer, too!"

"Fact that Swan didn't leave any estate might be an extenuating circumstance," Van Cleef suggested.

"I'm afraid not. It's a very serious matter, to destroy a will. If Downes is allowed to confess... My God! I—the possibility nearly drives me mad!"

"Are you mad?" thought Van Cleef.

"When I think of Emilia... in the dock... Emilia in prison..." said the Major, unsteadily, "I tell you frankly, sir, I could shoot that cowardly scoundrel who's responsible."

"That wouldn't help."

"It would," said the Major. "If Downes were out of the way, the thing would never come to light."

"What about Annie Downes?"

"She hasn't any evidence. Any statement she might make could be discredited as the slander of a jealous woman. And there's nothing to fear from Dulac, of course."

"You trust him?"

"Completely! In fact, it was he who warned me about Annie Downes. Came here to talk it over with me. Told me she'd taken up with the girl. He threatened Downes, too."

"With what?"

"With physical violence," said the Major. "Dulac, of course, knows nothing about the will. His only concern is to protect the girl from the disgrace of having the truth made public. He was alarmed when Annie Downes began asking her here."

They began walking again, silent for a time.

"Downes must be restrained," said the Major.

"Yes..." Van Cleef said, absently. There was so very much to think of now....

"We're both men of the world," the Major continued. "I can speak to you with candour. We both know that poor Emilia had no criminal intent, and that her action has had no detrimental effect upon anyone. Swan had left the house to Emilia, anyhow. The money he left to his daughter didn't exist. He'd squandered everything. But the legal criminality is undeniable. Downes has got to be restrained. And I see only one way to accomplish it."

"And what's that?"

"I tried this morning to buy him off," said Bramwell. "I'm by no means a rich man, but I'd have given him all I had. He refused. He's entirely in the—grip of his wife, and her one idea is to make Emilia suffer. Talks about 'conscience' and 'atonement.' The one idea she has is *vengeance*. I think that Downes was undoubtedly somewhat infatuated with Emilia. But she didn't know it. She never knows that." He was silent for a time. "And now, because of a vindictive woman's jealousy, she's in danger of—of utter ruin. It cannot be!"

"What d'you propose?"

"This was my idea," said the Major, in a half-apologetic tone. "I have no car, and if I hired one, it might seem suspicious. But this car of yours could be used in a perfectly natural way."

"Not mine, y'know. Belongs to Russell."

"It does? However, you came here in it. You could borrow it, in a perfectly natural way. You can ask Downes to come with you, on some pretext, and you meet me at some designated spot. The whole episode could be given the appearance of a hold-up, by motor-bandits."

"But—" said Van Cleef, in stupefaction.

"You're a man of the world!" cried the Major, desperately earnest. "We can arrange this between us. I can fire a shot or two at the car, afterwards."

"After—shooting Downes?"

"Exactly. You, of course, will claim to have been robbed. We can 'plant'—I believe that's the word—'plant' some of your possessions in a thicket—some place where the police will find them, as if dropped by the bandits in their flight. You'll say that Downes was killed, resisting the bandits."

"Needs quite a bit of thinking over..." said Van Cleef.

"Unfortunately, we have no time," said the Major. "It will have to be done at once, before Downes has an opportunity to go to the police. It ought to be done before lunch."

"No!" Van Cleef said to himself. "I'm insane myself. He can't possibly be saying what I imagine he's saying. That we've got to murder Downes before lunch.... He... No! *Look* at him! Ordinary, matter-of-fact man—smoking a cigar...."

"I don't want to hurry you—" said the Major, courteously. "But there's no time to spare."

"There might be a—better way out," said Van Cleef. "I mean to say—I don't quite like your plan."

"I dare say I'm old-fashioned," said the Major. "But it's my code, and always will be. I'd have no compunction whatever in shooting down any man who attempted to ruin a woman's reputation. Shooting him down like a dog!"

"My God!" thought Van Cleef. "I don't know.... I don't know anything.... Only that I've got to stop this...."

"Have you an alternative plan of action, sir?" the Major demanded.

"Working one out," Van Cleef answered. "Just wait a bit...."

They walked up and down, side by side. Anyone in the house could see them; perhaps Downes and his wife were looking at them. Two men of the world, discussing the murder of Harry Downes.... Ought to be done before lunch....

"I'll see Downes," said Van Cleef, abruptly.

"I've already seen him—"

"We'll give him one more chance," said Van Cleef, firmly. "I'll let you know at once...."

"I have little or no hope that you'll succeed," said the Major.

He remained, walking up and down the lawn, while Van Cleef went towards the house, with a purposeful air, and a stunned mind.

"See Downes..." he thought. "Offer him a bribe, to shut up? Suppose it's all a huge lie—an invention of Bramwell's? But he means business, all right. He's quite ready to shoot Downes 'like a dog.' Whatever else is true, that's clear. The mail's dangerous. I don't know whether or not he's insane. But he's dangerous. So what do I do about it? Go to the police? Then they hear this story about the will that was destroyed. If it's true, it's bad for Emilia. Damn bad. And it easily could be true.... She could have done that. She could go to jail for it. If I don't tell the police, then what? Shall I tell Robinson? He looks ethical. If he hears this will story, he probably wouldn't shut up...."

The front door was unlocked; he stepped into the hall, in a furtive, quiet way; he wanted to hide somewhere for a little time, while he thought. The drawing-room was empty; he went in there, and closed the door.

"One thing at a time," he told himself. "Chief thing now is, to keep Bramwell from shooting Downes. Apparently I'll have to do without the help of the police, or the medical profession. Can't get him locked up in jail or in an asylum, without bad consequences to Emilia. I've also got to keep Downes from confessing—if he really intends to, and if there's anything to confess."

He struck a match to light one of his eternal cigarettes, and his hand was shaking.

"Nervous," he thought, surprised. "I need a drink. No, Mr. Van Cleef, you need a clear head, for the next few hours.... Only you haven't got one." A footstep in the hall made him jump. And an idea came to him. He opened the door and went out into the hall, and there was Emilia.

"Hello!" he said, with a cheerful smile, and went past her, up the stairs, went to the Downes' room and knocked at the door. Annie Downes opened it.

"Like to speak to Harry..." he said.

"He's dozing," she answered, in a whisper. "Lizzy's accident upset him—"

"It's urgent," said Van Cleef, loudly, and Downes spoke:

"Come in, Arthur! Come in!"

He was lying on the bed, in a dressing-gown, and he looked just as usual.

"They all do," thought Van Cleef. "All the time! If they'd ever register anything.... Annie," he said, aloud, "if you don't mind, I want to speak to Harry alone."

"All right, Arthur!" she said, with an amiability he found suspicious. She picked up her knitting and went out.

"About Swan's will..." Van Cleef began.

Downes closed his eyes, in a look of suffering.

"Horrible..." he said. "If ever a man was punished for a moment's folly—"

"New development," said Van Cleef, very low, standing close to the bed. "The idea is, for you to come at once to see this fellow—"

"What fellow?" asked Downes, opening his eyes.

"Weatherby," said Van Cleef, without the slightest hesitation. "He's got hold of what he claims is another will—later one."

Downes put on his glasses and sat up.

"He wants us—you and me—to take a look at it—see if we can identify Bill's writing. It's a holograph will, y'see. All in his own hand."

"I don't understand this, Van Cleef. Who's this Weatherby, and where did he get hold of this document?"

"It's very mysterious," said Van Cleef. "Personally, I think he stole it. But if we think it's valid, Downes, we can buy it from him—at a price. This will makes no mention of anyone except Emilia, and, of course, it invalidates any former will. Or wills," he added, to make it more legal.

"I don't quite see—" Downes began.

"I'll explain, more fully," said Van Cleef. "But the great thing is haste. We must get in touch with Weatherby at once, before he—"

"Before what?"

All Van Cleef's inventiveness suddenly failed; for a moment he was speechless.

"You're a man of the world, Downes," he said, at last. "You'll understand, as soon as you meet him. But we've got to start at once. And the thing's got to be kept secret, for the moment. Better tell Annie the Chief of Police has sent for us, to answer some confidential questions."

"She won't believe that. I'll have to tell her the truth, Van Cleef."

"Impossible! I've given my word—"

"Van Cleef..." said Downes, unsteadily, "I can't get away from Annie without a very satisfactory explanation.... She's extremely intuitive. She—guesses things."

"We'll take her along, then," said Van Cleef, suddenly. "Explain to her, while you're dressing. I'll have a car here in ten minutes."

He went out of the room, closing the door behind him; he took out his handkerchief and wiped his forehead; he descended the stairs to the lounge and rang up a garage, to order a car. As he hung up the receiver, the Major spoke, at his shoulder.

"I see..." he said, very low. "Where shall I meet you, Van Cleef?"

"I'll handle this alone," said Van Cleef.

XII

The car came up the drive and stopped before the house, and someone sitting on the veranda in the dark rose.

"Is that you, Van Cleef, by any chance?"- asked a man's voice.

"Oh! Ross! Yes! Here I am!" answered Van Cleef. He handed a bill to the driver, and got a startled "Thank you!" in return; he mounted the steps. "So you're here, Ross!" he said.

"Naturally!" said Ross. "I told you this morning on the telephone that I'd come as early in the afternoon as possible. I've been here for over two hours."

"Two hours!" Van Cleef repeated, as if shocked. "Sorry."

"No one could tell me where you'd gone, or why. Or when you were likely to return. I was entirely at a loss."

"Sorry," Van Cleef repeated. "Suppose we go inside—" Because he wanted to look at Ross, with the old hope of learning something from his face.

"As you please," said Boss. "I'm obliged to stop here for dinner now, although I had an engagement."

He was offended, and he looked offended; a thin and distinguished man with a high-bridged nose and black hair turning grey. He kept on:

"I understand that you particularly wanted to see me, Mr. Van Cleef. Otherwise I'd have gone back to town as soon as I'd seen the police here, and made the necessary arrangements. I certainly understood, from your telephone conversation—"

"Very sorry, Ross. What about a drink?"

"I could do with one," said Ross.

They were shut into Van Cleef's room, and there would have to be an explanation.

"How much shall I tell Ross?" Van Cleef asked himself, as he poured out two drinks. "Water? How much? Well.... Here we are!"

They sipped their drinks in silence.

"The doctor who'd been attending Lizzy—Doctor—"

"Robinson."

"Doctor Robinson came here. He said you'd left a message at his house this morning that you wanted to see him."

"How much shall I tell him?" thought Van Cleef again, glancing again at that distinguished and disagreeable face. "That part of it, anyhow... I do want to see him," he said, aloud. "I wanted to ask him to—make a rather particular point of looking for any trace of poison."

"Someone's already been after him about that," said Ross, with what seemed to Van Cleef an inhuman indifference.

"What did Robinson say?"

"He's sending the organs to an analyst. He's the coroner's physician here, and he's more or less obliged to do so."

"You don't seem much bothered about the possibility of Lizzy's having been poisoned."

"I don't regard it as a possibility. I've seen this happen dozens of times before. In the shock of a sudden death, some hysterical friend or relative or servant will start talking about poison. The doctor assured me there was no superficial evidence of any poison. There's no imaginable motive for anyone's wishing to poison Lizzy. There's absolutely no reason to suspect poisoning. The only result of this hysteria is that the inquest will be delayed and the state will be put to unnecessary expense."

"Who spoke to Robinson about poison?"

"The house-boy. He had some garbled tale about your having been poisoned as well."

Van Cleef took another sip at his drink, and it occurred to him, suddenly, that for the first time in years it tasted good. It occurred to him that he had not particularly wanted it; that at seven o'clock he was having the first drink of the day....

"I can take it, or leave it..." he said to himself. "Maybe.... But there are more weighty matters at the moment.... How much shall I tell him?"

"What put the idea of poisoning into your mind?" asked Boss.

"I was probably hysterical," Van Cleef answered.

Boss glanced at him; their eyes met, and it was not a friendly glance.

"If you had, or have, any basis for suspicion, you would, of course, inform the police?"

"Of course," Van Cleef answered, and added to himself, "When I'm damn good and ready."

"Sergeant Warren was also here, asking for you," Boss went on. "He was very much annoyed that you and the Downses had all disappeared, without notifying him."

"Didn't disappear. Here I am."

"I advise you to telephone him, to say that you've returned, and to tell him where he can reach Downes."

"What does he want to reach Downes for?"

"He may be wanted at the inquest."

"Well, you said the inquest would be delayed. Downes will turn up."

"Van Cleef," said Ross, "you've put me in an embarrassing and humiliating position. You ask me to come here, to meet you, and discuss Lizzy's affairs. I come, and you've disappeared, without leaving any message for me."

"You'd have had to come, though, in any case, wouldn't you? She was your client."

"That's not to the point. You're also a client of mine. And you are not showing the necessary confidence in me. You are concealing things from me, Van Cleef."

"I'm not being a client at the moment, if you know what I mean," said Van Cleef, apologetically.

"You mean, I take it, that you do not want me to represent your interests in this case."

"If it is a case."

"Van Cleef.... As a friend of Lizzy Carroll's, have you any information which should be given to me?"

"I don't know," said Van Cleef. "That's a fact. I don't know whether what I've got is 'information' or not. But I'll know better to-morrow."

"You're willing to assume the responsibility of withholding what may be important information?"

"Another drink, Ross?"

"Thank you."

Van Cleef stood with the bottle in his hand.

"Can I do without another drink? Excellent!" he thought.

"I advise you, however, to notify the police immediately as to Downes's whereabouts."

Van Cleef stared at him, his face tense and stiff with the effort not to laugh.

"Very likely it's not funny, anyhow," he told himself. He tried not to picture Annie and Harry Downes.... They were at the moment sitting in a room he had engaged for them in his New York hotel; they were waiting for a telephone message from "Weatherby."

"It may be late," Van Cleef had warned them. "Lot of complications.... If the call's delayed—you could have dinner sent up.... You could turn in, and sleep for a bit, if the call was—very much delayed...."

It had taken a great deal of persuasion to get them there, and a great deal of ingenuity. Mrs. Downes clung to the idea that her husband should confess his guilt to the police. She had strange quasi-legal arguments for this; the courts, she said, are always lenient toward people who *volunteer* information. It was much better, she held, to explain the whole thing to the police before they found it out for themselves.

"And now, of course, with the police in the house, investigating about poor Lizzy, they're sure to find out," she had said.

"Shouldn't say sure, by any means," Van Cleef had protested.

But she wanted to believe that. She was trying to disguise, even from herself, her bitter desire to see Emilia disgraced.

"I'm sure," she kept saying, "that if Harry tells the police now, there'll be no unpleasantness. Everyone will understand that Emilia wasn't herself." And when that hadn't worked: "I do think," she had said, "that it's a dreadful injustice to Blanche. Bill wanted to acknowledge her. She really has a right to know who she is."

Van Cleef felt that he had done well. He had talked to Annie alone; he too had been legal; he had assured her that Downes would lose all civil rights.

"What does that mean?" she had asked.

His explanation had been vague, but alarming. He had also talked about what prison would do to Harry Downes's health, and he had assured her that a confession would inevitably mean prison. He had made an impression on her, and a night to think it over, a night without the sight of Emilia, would deepen the impression. But his chief object had been to gain time. He had had to get Downes away from the Major and his gun; he had had to get both the Downeses away from the police, before they could talk.

What he now had to do was to work over the Major, convince him that Downes was no longer a menace to Emilia, to pacify him.

"I think it can be done," he said to himself. "He's not what you'd call clever. But he's not crazy. His idea for killing Downes wasn't crazy. It was stupid. Brutal, if you like. But not insane. It simply looked to him like the one way to protect Emilia. *If* Downes and myself were poisoned, he didn't do it. That's not the way he'd take."

If there was a poisoner, who was it? He had thought that over all the way home in the hired car. He ruled out the Major, and Lizzy Carroll, and, that done, he could make out a good enough case against everyone else in the house. Downes was his favourite. Downes had tried to commit suicide, and, failing in that, had tried to kill Van Cleef, because he was Emilia's friend. After Downes then Emilia, Russell, Harly, and Dulac, in that order.

"It's a psychological grading," he thought. "It'll do, for the time being. And if the doctors find that Lizzy wasn't poisoned, that's the finish. I'll get Emilia away from here, scatter this crew, and that's the finish. Important thing is, to keep everything quiet until we know about poor Lizzy."

No use thinking beyond that now. And no use thinking too much about the warning Blanche had got.

"Might be some boy-friend of hers," he thought. "Someone entirely outside the rest of it."

She must have boy-friends. She must have a life of which he knew nothing, never would know anything. He hoped she wouldn't have to know about Bill Swan. He hoped nothing would hurt her, much. She was too honest and too kind not to be hurt at all, but he hoped it would never be much....

"I shan't be seeing her again," he thought. "Only makes trouble for her."

Ross cleared his throat.

"There were two or three reporters here," he said. "I gave them a brief statement. I said Miss Carroll had fallen from the balcony, during a heart attack. I also sent a cable to her nephew in London, and to an old friend of hers in Mexico. There were only three people she wanted notified in case of her death. You were the third."

"I?" said Van Cleef, and was silent for a time. "We never saw much of each other," he said. "Never were intimate. Only—I liked her."—

"Apparently she liked you," said Ross. He held up his glass and stared at it. "Mrs. Swan's attitude is—peculiar," he observed.

"Very highly-strung."

"Quite. The Sergeant and Doctor Robinson both told me she'd been insistent at first that the death was a suicide."

"Oh, yes! That's natural."

"Why is it natural?"

"Y'see," Van Cleef explained, "Emilia felt responsible for the condition of the balcony. Very sensitive about things like that."

"Hmm..." said Ross, glancing at him. "I'm also informed that she suggested Lizzy had been addicted to drugs."

"Same idea. Panic-stricken attempt to evade responsibility for the condition of the balcony."

"Scarcely admirable..." said Ross.

"She took it all back. It was nothing but an impulse—self-preservation...."

"Hmm..." said Ross, again. "Well, I'll be leaving after dinner, Van Cleef. We'd better discuss matters at once."

"Yes. Arrangements for the funeral—"

"Is that all you wanted to discuss?"

"That's all," said Van Cleef, sure now that he did not care to tell Ross about the Major, about Downes, above all, about Emilia.

"Who's the boy?" asked Ross, abruptly.

"Name of Russell Blackman. I used to know his people, years ago."

"What's he doing here?"

"Drove me out. Doesn't know what to do with himself."

"Van Cleef, if I were you, I'd get rid of him."

"Gets under your skin, doesn't he?" said Van Cleef, with a smile.

"I've met his type before," said Ross. "They're always potentially dangerous."

"What way?"

"I had a talk with him. Or I might better say, he had a talk with me. He has a well-marked delusion of persecution."

Van Cleef heard that with surprise, and a slow-dawning amusement.

"The biter bit," he thought. "Exactly what Russell said about the Major.... These amateur psychologists are all so positive. Warning you...."

"I'm not joking," said Ross, glancing at Van Cleef's face. "The boy is convinced that everyone's against him."

"Not a delusion, though," said Van Cleef. "It's a fact. Pretty well everyone is against him. That's the effect he has on people."

"The cause of—" A knock at the door interrupted Ross; it was Emilia, in a dress of dark purple wool, cut square at the base of her throat, with short puff sleeves; she was anxious, appealing, and altogether beautiful.

"Are you ready for dinner?" she asked. "Harly's rather late, I'm afraid...."

It was a strange dinner, almost macabre. Emilia had Ross and Van Cleef at the table with her; the Major sat alone at one small table, and Russell at another; nobody spoke to either of them.

"I wonder..." thought Van Cleef. "I wonder what's in Bramwell's mind, just now? Does he imagine I've done away with Downes—both the Downeses? Could he sit there, eating his dinner, if he believed that? If he'd done it himself, how would he behave? Is he sane, after all, to propose a murder in a perfectly matter-of-fact way? Or am I the morbid one? He saw the deed as a practical necessity, that's all...."

Emilia spoke to him; he turned towards her and engaged in conversation. But his attention wandered; he glanced again at those two who sat, each alone and disregarded, at his little table.

"Both having delusions?" he thought.

It was a cool and breezy night; the trees rustled incessantly, the curtain on the window near him stirred back and forth against the screen with a faint rasping sound. Harly moved about quietly.

"Ross doesn't like Emilia," Van Cleef thought. "Do I? Yes, I don't know why."

Ross was speaking:

"Then if you'll excuse me, Mrs. Swan? I've ordered a taxi to take me to the train.... One or two matters to discuss with Van Cleef...."

They went up to Van Cleef's room again.

"The inquest will be held as soon as the reports of the autopsy are completed," said Ross. "Then I hope there'll be an end to this—" He paused. "This most unpleasant affair.... This unnecessary and most unpleasant affair...."

"Yes..."

"I advise you once more, Van Cleef, to get in touch with the Sergeant, in regard to Downes."

"Thanks."

"Any sort of unusual behaviour will, naturally, give colour to these preposterous and utterly unfounded rumours," said Ross, with a sudden irritability. "These rumours.... An insult against Miss Carroll's memory.... And utterly unfounded."

"You're worried," thought Van Cleef, with uneasiness. They had little more to say; in half an hour or so, Ross left, and Van Cleef remained in his room, disinclined to talk to anyone. "Rumours..." he thought. "Ever since I came out here, I've been listening to rumours.... Blackmail... poisoning... delusions.... Is it all unfounded? I wish to God I knew. Almost anything would be better than this cloudiness.... Has there been any crime? Any murder?"

He sighed, and lit another cigarette, walked up and down his room. He thought of Lizzy Carroll, and he thought of Blanche; he thought of Emilia.

"I'll have to suggest that idea to her," he thought. "Idea that she was panic-stricken about the condition of the balcony. It's a good one for her."

He heard a shot. Loud, sharp, somewhere near him, somewhere inside the house. He stood as if stunned, until he heard running footsteps in the hall.

"It's happened..." he said, aloud. And felt that he had been waiting for this shattering sound, this open violence.

XIII

It was Harly who had gone running by; he was standing across the corridor now, outside the Major's door.

"I heard a shot, sir," he said, looking over his shoulder at Van Cleef.

"In there, d'you think? Knock...."

Harly knocked.

"Well?" answered Bramwell. Or someone imitating Bramwell, in a shaking, falsetto voice. "What d'you want?"

"Mind opening the door just a moment?" asked Van Cleef. And now Emilia was beside him, clutching his arm.

"I—I do mind!" said Bramwell. "Kindly let me alone...."

"Aa-rthur...."

"Hush!" he said to her. "Bramwell, just a moment—"

"Go to hell!" said the Major.

"Arthur.... Was that a shot?"

Russell had come out of his room; he stood leaning against his closed door, sullen and still.

"Bramwell," said Van Cleef. "Mrs. Swan's worried. Open the door, will you?"

"I won't. I'm—in bed. Get out, and let me alone, if you please!"

"Carlo! Are you all right?" she cried.

"Yes! Entirely all right! I want—to be *let alone!*" he shouted.

"Perhaps—" Van Cleef began, when Russell took a step forward.

"Look!" he said.

Van Cleef looked where he pointed; he saw the little thread of blood running from under Bramwell's door.

"Emilia," he said. "Go into your own room for a while, will you?"

"No..." she said. "I don't want—"

"Come, my dear girl," he interrupted, taking her by the elbow. He wanted to speak kindly, he wanted to feel kindly towards her, but there was in him only an exasperated impatience to get her out of the way.

"Please, Arthur.... I don't want—to stay alone...."

"Only for a few moments," he said. He tried to draw her forward, but she resisted. He could not drag her; there was no time to persuade her. "Russell," he said, "look after Mrs. Swan, will you?" He took her hand from his arm and raised his voice. "Open that door, Bramwell!"

No answer this time. Never any answer again, perhaps. He moved to the next door, the door of the room that had been Lizzy Carroll's; he tried it, and it was locked.

"We'll have to break in his door," he said to Harly.

Emilia was beside him again, clutching his arm again.

"Arthur, why? Arthur, what's happened?"

"Russell, *can't* you look after Mrs. Swan?" he shouted. "Harly, get an axe—"

"I have a key—for Lizzy's door, Arthur...."

"Good! Will you get it, please?"

"It's here," she said, and tried to open her purse with shaking fingers. She brought out a key at last, and dropped it; he picked it up.

"Wait-in my room—anywhere you like," he said. "Russell will stay with you."

But Russell did not say a word, did not move; he stood leaning against his door, sullen and still.

"Harly—look after Mrs. Swan," said Van Cleef, and unlocked Lizzy Carroll's door. The room was in blackness, with a strong, cool current of air blowing through it; he felt for the switch, and turned it, but no light came. The window made a pale square; he moved across the room towards it.

"Shot himself," he thought. "Why? Because he's mad? Shot himself—but maybe he's not dead...."

When he reached the window, the world outside seemed almost light; the unclouded sky was thick with stars. He saw the gap in the iron railing, saw the boards splintered and sagging. He set foot on it cautiously; when he got out there, he saw brilliant light shining from the Major's window. And he heard, or thought he heard, the sound of difficult breathing. He edged along, keeping close to the wall; he went very slowly, testing each step, and he was filled with a peculiar nervous fear completely new to him. He remembered the mare he used to ride, and how she had always balked at a wooden bridge, sometimes becoming unmanageable, sometimes consenting, stepping across the planks with a trembling, unsteady gait.

"Felt like this," he thought. "You think the thing'll give way under you.... I'm glad Lizzy—didn't know...."

He had got to the Major's window; he stepped upon the low sill with a sigh of relief. The room was brightly lit, by two lamps, and a chandelier in the ceiling, and lying near the door was a man. Not Bramwell. It was Dulac, shot through the head.

There was no need to touch him. No need to look at him V again. He was dead, brutally dead, shattered. Van Cleef stared down at his own feet for a moment....

"Pull yourself together..." he said in his heart. "*Where's Bramwell?*"

He raised his head, as if someone else had asked him that question; he looked about the bright room, every corner of it visible. And he heard, or thought he heard, the sound of difficult breathing. It was not Dulac. It did not come from inside the room. So it had to be on the balcony. He stepped into the room.

"Bramwell must have a gun," he thought. "And he must be mad."

No one in the house now but himself, Russell, Harly, and Emilia. And Bramwell crouched on the balcony, outside the bar of light from the window. He crossed the room to the door; and he had to move Dulac.... He unlocked the door, took out the key, opened it, and stepped into the corridor; he locked the door behind him.

"Aa-rthur!" cried Emilia. "Blood—on your *hands*!"

He caught her before she fell, lifted her and carried her into his room, where he laid her on the bed.

"Stay with Mrs. Swan, Harly," he said. "Lock the door on the inside. Lock the window, too."

Russell still stood there, motionless.

"Look here!" said Van Cleef. "There's been a murder. Dulac. Go down, will you, and call up the police."

"What are you going to do?"

I'm pretty sure Bramwell's on the balcony. I'll go round there and see if he comes down."

"I'll do that," said Russell, and took a small automatic out of his hip pocket. He smiled. "I'll wait for the Major, and you can telephone."

"Better give me that," said Van Cleef.

Russell dropped the automatic into his pocket again.

"Give it to me," said Van Cleef.

"Why the hell should I?" cried Russell. "I won't—"

"Shut up and give it to me."

"I will not!"

Van Cleef thought for a moment, staring at the boy with a frown. Then he acted very quickly. He gave the boy a short right to the jaw that jerked his head back, caught his arm and pulled it up, and took the gun out of his pocket.

"Telephone to the police," he said, briefly, and turning away, ran down the stairs. The front door was unbolted; he opened it and stepped out on the veranda. It was a sweet, cool night, so quiet.

"Mad..." he thought. "Homicidal.... Likes to kill.... Did he kill Lizzy?"

Walking silently on the grass, he turned the corner of the house, and he saw a figure hanging to the edge of the balcony by its hands.

"Bramwell," he called, as quietly, as reasonably as he could.

The figure dropped to the ground and began to run towards a plantation of trees that stood on the lawn, a sharply-defined octagon of black. Van Cleef started after him, and stopped.

"He's got a gun, and he's mad. No use being a fool...."

He drew close to the house, in the shadow, and went forward cautiously. But he could not reach the trees without crossing a clear space; he stopped again; he could see nothing in the plantation, but he heard things stir, things rustle; he heard a twig snap.

"Bramwell!" he called persuasively. "Let's talk this over."

No answer. He heard a twig snap, a branch rustle as if thrust aside, and the sounds were farther from him now.

"I'll take a chance," he thought, and ran across the clear space, to the shelter of the trees. He listened, tense, alert, alive; it was a sort of exultation to be so alive. "If I could get up behind him..." he thought, listening for another sound. Very dark here among the trees, very still. He moved forward, listened, took another step. And heard that breathing. He grinned to himself, moving stealthily nearer.

"Where are you, Van Cleef?" called Russell's voice.

There was a scrambling, crashing sound, a swishing of leaves.

"He's off, down the lawn!" yelled Russell.

Van Cleef got out of the little wood, and then he saw Bramwell, big and square, charging over the grass towards the wall, with Russell after him. He ran after them; he was gaining on them; the boy wasn't much of a runner. The Major I reached the wall and flung himself over it, clumsily, almost in front of a car that came round the corner. It stopped with a screech from the brakes.

"What the hell—!" cried the driver.

"We're after that man!" called Russell. "A murderer—"

"Someone up at Mrs. Swan's?"

"That's right!" said Russell.

The driver got out; he was standing in the road when Van Cleef joined them. Bramwell was nowhere in sight. Across the road there was a barn, a field with a white wooden fence, and in the background a little old farmhouse.

"Has to be in the barn," said Van Cleef.

They all three crossed the road together, and again it was Russell who sighted the quarry.

"He's got out! There he goes!"

There he went, running across the empty field, towards the house. Van Cleef was climbing the fence when the driver drew in his breath with a sort of hiss.

"Jeeze!"

The Major turned and started back towards them, and after him came a huge dog, loping silently in the starlight. The Major looked back over his shoulder, and seeing the dog so close, gave a yell. He made a desperate spurt forward; he stumbled and fell, and the dog was on him. Van Cleef heard that sound that has meant the extremity of terror to man since his beginning. A beast worrying his prey.

He got over the fence, and took aim; as the shot rang out, the dog leaped into the air, and came running at him. He fired again, and it dropped. Bramwell was on his feet again, running, bent over, not like a man any more. Like a beast, hunted by beasts.

"Bramwell!" cried Van Cleef. "For God's sake, man!"

A beast himself gone back ten thousand years in time, to have felt that atrocious exultation.

"Bramwell!"

He wanted some way to reach him, to reassure him. But Bramwell fell on his face and lay still.

The driver had an electric torch; Van Cleef turned the Major over, and the light shone on him.

"Got the throat half torn out of him..." said the driver, in a sort of awe. "You wouldn't think he could have kept going—"

A light sprang up in the farmhouse, a shaking old voice shouted from an upper window.

"What's all this?"

"It's me, Mr. Horton!" called the driver. "We caught this here murderer...."

"Van Cleef..." said Russell, putting a hand on his shoulder. Van Cleef shook him off.

"Got a telephone?" he called to the man at the window. "Then call Doctor Robinson, will you, and the police!"

"Van Cleef..." said Russell again, and leaned weakly against him. "I'm going to be sick...."

Van Cleef pushed him away, gently, absently, not interested. The boy was being sick, horribly sick; the driver was murmuring phrases of encouragement to him. But Van Cleef stood erect, beside the Major, waiting for him to die.

Not dead yet; the breath whistled in his torn throat. He lay there, in the dark, empty field, and wouldn't die. He had been hunted and harried; this was his last chance to escape, and he was not taking it. If he didn't go now, there would be worse things ahead of him.

"Let him go!" Van Cleef said to himself, in a sort of prayer. "He's had enough, poor devil...."

The wail of a siren startled him. It didn't seem possible that the police could come so soon. But perhaps he had lost track of time. Turning his head, he saw two cars come tearing along the road and stop; saw four or five dark figures jump out, come hastily towards him, with electric torches.

"Where's the man who was shot?" asked a serious young voice.

"Here!" he answered. "Not shot, though."

Two men were carrying a stretcher; the light of powerful torches shone on the prostrate man.

"God!" said the serious young voice. "This is..." He knelt beside Bramwell. "Funny..." he said. "When we got back from a call, there was this message. 'Man shot near Horton's barn.

Van Cleef moved aside, out of the radius of light.

"I see..." he said, after a moment. "I see...."

XIV

They put the man who wouldn't die on the stretcher; he wore a bandage like a very high collar that gave him a grotesquely formal look; they carried him off to the ambulance. "We'll go along up to the house now," said Sergeant Warren. "Get an account of all this."

"There's a—a—corpse in the house," said Russell, with a slight stammer.

"That so?" said the Sergeant, unmoved. "We'll take that up, when we get there." He stood, flanked by two policemen, obviously waiting, and Van Cleef touched the boy's arm. "Come on!" he said.

They set off across the field together, the Sergeant and the two policemen behind them.

"How are you feeling now?" asked Van Cleef.

"Fine!" Russell answered. "It was just the excitement...."

"Yes...." He lowered his voice. "This is the last chance we'll have, to talk alone."

"What d'you mean?"

"The last chance," he repeated. "Y'see, I *know*."

There was a silence.

"What do you think you know?" Russell asked, scornfully.

"I know who killed Lizzy Carroll, and Dulac, and Bramwell."

"Bramwell killed Miss Carroll and Dulac, and a dog killed him."

"No."

"You'll find that the police will agree with me."

"Wasn't thinking of the police, at the moment."

Again they were silent for a time; they reached the road where the police car stood, making a bright river of light that flowed over white dust, green grass, quiet trees.

"I ought to have seen, from the start..." said Van Cleef. "It's my fault...."

"Seen what? My little plan? Nobody could have seen through it. It's been fool-proof."

"One error. One serious error. You telephoned the police that a man had been shot near the barn. Telephoned a bit too soon."

"That's easily covered. I didn't telephone myself. I made Harly do it. He said what I told him, but I can always deny that. I can say he got mixed up. Nobody'll take his word against *mine*."

"You're going to fight this?"

"There's nothing to fight," said Russell, with a light laugh.

There's absolutely nothing against me. Surmises and suspicions won't count. The case against Bramwell's perfect."

"I'd like to know about Lizzy..." said Van Cleef.

"I'll tell you, then. You can't use it. I'm glad of a chance to tell you. I knew you were fond of her. She wasn't intended to die."

"Just to get indigestion, same as Downes and myself?"

"That was the idea. After she'd said good night to you, she was upset. She was sitting in her room, reading, with her door open, and two big pitchers of water on the floor beside her."

"Yes," Van Cleef said, half to himself. "Afraid I'd set the house on fire."

"She was glad to see me, and have a chat," said Russell. "When I suggested making tea, she was pleased. I went down into the kitchen and made it, and brought it up, all ready for her. What I gave her wouldn't have done any harm, if she hadn't had that cardiac condition. I didn't know anything about that, of course. We had our tea, very cosily, then I carried the tray downstairs. When I came back, she was dead."

"A—an easy way to go?"

"As easy as falling asleep. I was sorry, but I wanted to turn the accident to advantage. I decided that she had better be found on the balcony outside the Major's window. I was carrying her there, holding the railing to steady myself, when the damned thing began to crumble. I just saved myself, but I had to let her go. That pretty well spoiled the whole thing. I couldn't see how her death could be linked up with Bramwell."

"How would you have linked up the 'indigestion' with Bramwell?"

"Elementary, my dear Watson! She had a thermos jug of water there; she told me she made a habit of drinking— I forget how many glasses of water at night. Poison would have been found in the thermos jug. The Major's room was next to hers. The Major had suffered acutely from her radio, and from her tongue."

They were on the lawn now; there were lights in the house before them.

"About Bill Swan?"

"I don't know any more about Bill Swan's death than you do. That was just an artistic touch."

"Was Downes meant to die?"

"No. Downes was simply a demonstration. If you'd believed in him, it would have been the end."

"Not quite clear." Van Cleef slackened his pace; there was no sound behind him; he did not know how close the Sergeant and his two men might be, or how much they could hear, and he dared not look.

"I wanted to make you realize what I am!" said Russell steadily. "I hoped you'd take that episode at face value, hoped you'd believe I had the skill to save the man's life, and the brains to solve a mystery. If you had believed it, there'd have been no need to go on. You'd have accepted me as an equal. I shouldn't have needed to—" He paused. "To show off any more," he said, with a sigh.

"Show off..." Van Cleef repeated.

"That's what it amounts to," said Russell. "Ever since I was a kid, I've had it in my mind—that some day I'd make an impression on you. It's been easy to impress other people. But you were damned obstinate. Even when I gave you a dose yourself, you weren't convinced. So I had to go on. I had to make a first-class thriller out of it. I had to make a better case against Bramwell, for myself to solve."

"Was Dulac an accident?"

"No. He was carefully planned. He got a telephone message, asking him to see Bramwell at a certain time. He'd been to the house before, to see Downes; I found that out from Harly, and he was in a rage at Downes, I don't quite know why. Downes wanted to tell something that Dulac didn't want known. The voice on the telephone asked him to see Bramwell about 'the Downes affair' and asked him to come up by way of the balcony. He was one of those athletic old boys who like to show how nimble they are. He came, and he climbed up, and I was waiting. I gave it to him just as he reached the window."

They were close to the house now.

"If Bramwell hadn't played into your hands, you'd have been in a spot," said Van Cleef. "Curious way for him to behave."

"Not at all curious," said Russell. "Ten minutes before Dulac arrived, there was a note pushed under the Major's door. Typed. Signed, Emilia. Emilia wrote her gallant Major that Dulac was threatening her, and that she was going to have a final interview with him, and then flee. She asked the Major to meet her in Horton's barn at exactly half-past-nine. I knew it was the sort of note to appeal to him. I knew he'd think that *she'd* shot Dulac, and he'd be delighted to assume the guilt."

"Still, the message to the police that Bramwell had been shot was a bit of a mistake...."

"Yes..." Russell admitted, reluctantly. "I did lose my head, a little. You see, if you hadn't taken my gun, he would have been shot. The whole thing was so vivid, in my mind.... Just as I'd planned it.... I'd seen Horton's dog, and made enquiries about it. When I led everyone to the barn, he'd try to escape by the back, and he'd meet the dog. And I'd shoot at the dog, but I'd hit Bramwell first, by mistake. I did lose my head, for a moment.... It's the only mistake I've made. And it's understandable enough.... The idea of a man-hunt had me pretty worked up."

They had reached the veranda steps.

"You sent that note to Blanche?"

"Yes. She makes me sick.... I could see you falling for that, naive, miller's-daughter stuff.... I wanted to stop it, if I could."

Now Van Cleef looked back, and the Sergeant and his men were only a few paces from them.

"Russell..." he said. "Do you want your gun—now?"

Not a sound from the house. The trees rustled in the light wind, an insect chirped briskly.

"You mean...?" said Russell.

"Yes. Last chance."

Everything so quiet....

"Come along, please," said the Sergeant.

"No!" cried the boy, "I'm not worrying. I'm all right."

They all went up the steps together, they entered the house, and, in the lighted hall, Van Cleef looked at Russell. His dark face had a slightly dazed look, a look of wonder that gave it a terrible innocence. The innocence of a very young devil, who had not tasted of the fruit of knowledge, but knew only evil. A devil, shut out of hell where he belonged, and set down in a world of human creatures who rejected him. They all rejected him, all.

The Sergeant looked on, like a calm idol, while those two faced each other with that long glance.

"Where's the body, Mr. Van Cleef?" he asked, at last.

"Upstairs. In Bramwell's room."

"I'll ask you and this boy to wait here in the hall while I take a look. Kelly, remain here."

"Yes, sir," said one of the policemen.

He was there, to hear all they might say. The last time, the last chance had gone.

"If I'd understood in time..." thought Van Cleef. "If I'd even tried to understand.... Lizzy might still be here. And Bramwell.... I didn't try.... *Mea culpa.... Mea maxima culpa....*"

XV

"I told you at the time," said Ross, "that the boy was dangerous. Delusion of persecution."

"I told you he *was* persecuted," said Van Cleef, with unusual energy. "You couldn't help persecuting him. Something about him that antagonized everyone."

"That, of course, was because of his defensive attitude. Convinced, as he was, that—"

"You don't know," Van Cleef interrupted. "Nobody knows."

"Any competent alienist knows."

"What does this bird say?"

"Von Felder? He says that even now, after only one interview with the boy, he's prepared to state definitely that he's a psychopathic personality."

"Meaning crazy?"

"Exactly. Definitely—and incurably—insane."

"What happens about it?"

"I doubt," said Ross, "if he'll ever be brought to trial. I think that in all probability there'll be a commission appointed to examine him, and declare him incompetent."

"And then what? Strait-jacket and padded cell?"

"Surely you know better than that," said Ross, annoyed. "You know that in a modern institution he'll get such treatment as his condition requires."

"Same thing," said Van Cleef. "He'll make baskets. Much better to hang him."

Ross said nothing to that; they sat facing each other in the drawing-room, both smoking, both irritated. Ross glanced at his watch.

"Mrs. Swan is taking all this very well. Very well indeed," he observed.

"Love," said Van Cleef.

This flippancy still further irritated Ross; he stirred restlessly. He repeated the offensive word.

"Love? For Bramwell?"

"Oh, yes!"

"He didn't impress me as a man of any particular intelligence or personality."

"He's got what it takes," said Van Cleef.

"He has extraordinary vitality," said Ross. "Doctor Robinson says that not one man in a thousand could have survived such an ordeal."

Van Cleef stopped listening to him. He had seen Bramwell that morning in the hospital, Bramwell with that bandage like a very high collar, his ruddy face grown pallid. He had obviously been in pain, and be could not speak, would not be able to speak for days, and never again much above a whisper. But his blue eyes still had that stupid and honest glance; he was still alive.

"Hell never understand what's happened to him," Van Cleef thought. "They'll talk to him about Russell's psychopathic personality and so on...."

Emilia had been sitting in the hospital room with him. Just sitting there, getting up now and then, to pat his pillow, smooth the bed, adjust the blind; and his eyes followed her with devotion.

"Possibly the one man on earth who'd never be exasperated by her," Van Cleef thought. "Poor girl! She'll marry him, and they'll be happy. She has this house, and he has his little income.... They'll both be able to forget. The balcony will be repaired, and they'll never, never see Lizzy standing there. They'll never stop outside the door of Bramwell's room because Dulac's lying there again. No ghosts.... Bill Swan's ghost never came back here. Emilia wouldn't encourage it."

He was waiting now, with Boss, for a little lunch offered them by Emilia; after that, they were going back to town together. A woman from the village had come to stay with Emilia in her empty house; only she and Harly would be left, of the eight who had been here twenty-four hours ago. Would she sit alone in the dining-room to-night...?

A car was coming up the drive.

"The police have been remarkably efficient in handling the newspaper men," said Boss, uneasily. "I hope—"

The doorbell rang.

"There'll be a great deal of publicity, though," he went on. "It can't be avoided. It's a remarkably sensational case."

"Front-page stuff."

"As you say, front-page stuff. And I'm afraid you'll figure in it, Van Cleef." He waited, but there was no reply, and a sort of remorse came over him. "You're looking rather seedy, Van Cleef."

"I feel seedy. That's because I *don't* need a drink."

Harly went along the hall to open the door.

"You can't—" Boss began, when Harry and Annie Downes came into the room. Van Cleef rose, with guilty alarm; he smiled at them. And they both smiled at him; they were just the same—the middle-aged couple with eye-glasses that he met everywhere....

"Annie, this is Mr. Ross, Lizzy's lawyer, and mine.... Downes, Mr. Ross...."

Annie sat down and took off her gloves.

"I called up the house, and Harly told me..." she said, in a hushed voice. "So terrible.... I—we thought we ought to come back, to be with Emilia until it's all over...."

Telephone, Mr. Ross, sir," said Harly, and Ross went out of the room. Van Cleef was left alone with the couple he had deluded; they must know now that they had been deluded.

"How did you make out?" he asked.

"Harry saw Mr. Weatherby, late last night," said Mrs. Downes. "And he was quite convinced that this other will is genuine."

"I see!" said Van Cleef. He could not help going on. "What did you think of Weatherby, Downes?"

"Oh.... A gentleman," said Downes.

"In every sense of the word," said Van Cleef.

"Yes," said Downes, gravely. "In every sense of the word."

"Does Annie believe that he really saw a Weatherby?" thought Van Cleef. "Or is she pretending, because she wants to drop the revenge motif? Or did I make a Weatherby materialize?"

"We stopped—" said Annie Downes, in a whisper, "we stopped to speak to poor little Blanche. We thought she ought to know the *truth*."

"You told her—"

"We felt that she ought to know, before Dulac's funeral," said Downes. "Ought to know he was not her father. Otherwise, it's making a mockery of—" He paused. "Of a—very solemn thing," he said.

"I'll be back," said Van Cleef.

He almost collided with Ross who was re-entering the room.

"I'll be back," he explained, and telephoned for a taxi; took up his hat, and walked down the drive to wait for it. Two policemen were stationed there; two photographers had cameras set up on tripods, and they got him as he passed.

"Millionaire Playboy leaving Murder House.... I may be followed.... All right! I'm buying cigarettes.... It was only right to tell her.... To knock her on the head.... To spoil all she can remember of her mother.... To undo all that Dulac tried to do...."The cab came, and he got into it; he drove to the shop, but she was not there.

"I might have known that," he thought.

A stout woman in a black wig was behind the counter.

"Will you let me have Miss Dulac's address?" he asked.

"No, I won't," she said, "It's a sin and a shame the way you people bother her."

"I'm not from a newspaper. I'm a friend—"

"No, you're not!" said she.

"Will you ring her up and tell her Arthur Van Cleef wants to say good-bye?"

"She doesn't want to see anybody, poor child. With her father not in his grave yet."

"Will you just ask her?"

The woman looked at him with her little black eyes.

"All right! I'll *ask* her," she said, "Wait here."

She disappeared through the door at the back of the shop. A customer came in, and stared at Van Cleef, waited, rapped on the counter with a coin; then he grew angry, and walked out. It was a good ten minutes before the woman returned.

"You can go right up," she said, with a sort of gentleness. "She's staying here with us for a while."

He went up a dark and narrow flight of stairs to a crowded little sitting-room, hot in the noon sun. Blanche was standing, waiting for him. She had obviously been crying; her face was tear-stained and sad. But not tragic.

"I hoped you'd come," she said.

"Mrs. Downes said she'd—seen you...."

"Yes," she said, and turned away her head. With a strangely comprehensive glance, Van Cleef noticed the details of the room; an upright piano covered by a blue velvet scarf fringed with gold, a little rug before the hearth, with a St. Bernard dog woven in it; a round table with a marble top, upon which stood two bronze houris designed to serve as bookends, but idle now. A neat, clean room, smelling of cabbage....

"Mrs. Downes told me," she said.

"I'm sorry."

"Well, no..." she said. "I guess it's always better to know the truth. I—" Her voice grew unsteady; she stopped for a moment. "It doesn't—really make any difference," she said. "I'm going to keep on thinking of him—as my father.... And if he could—forgive mother—and go on liking me..."

He found nothing to say.

"You look terribly tired," she said.

"I haven't had a drink for a long time," he said, smiling. "That's nothing," said she.

"I wanted a little praise...."

"You never had to drink," she said. "I mean, it was just psychological—"

"I don't think I believe in psychology."

"Oh!" she protested, shocked. Their eyes met. "I mean," he explained, "I don't like psychology."

"I see!"

They were both embarrassed, ill at ease. "I didn't—" he said. "I couldn't leave without saying good-bye."

"Well, but does it have to be good-bye?" she asked. The question astounded him. He could think of a good many answers....

"*Au revoir*," she said, resolutely, and held out her hand. He took it, in a quick grasp, and let it go.

"Maybe you're right..." he said. "*Au revoir!*"